The Heart That Lingers

JUNE MASTERS BACHER

HARVEST HOUSE PUBLISHERS, INC.
Eugene, Oregon 97402

Other Rhapsody Romance Books:

If Love Be Ours
Another Love *(Coming Fall 1989)*
With All My Heart *(Coming Fall 1989)*

THE HEART THAT LINGERS

Copyright © 1983 Harvest House Publishers, Inc.
Eugene, Oregon 97402

ISBN 0-89081-398-1

Printed in the United States of America.

Dedicated
to
each person whose path
has crossed mine.
You are the sum of these pages,
for mine is
THE HEART THAT LINGERS.

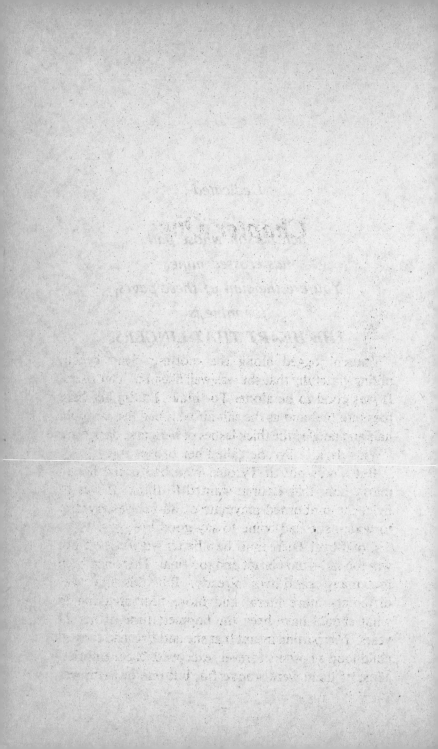

Chapter One

Lauren jogged along the morning-clean beach, noting gratefully that she was well ahead of later risers. It was good to be alone. To think. To dig her bare toes into the sand as the salt air whipped her ash-gold hair and tangled the thick lashes of her dark, dark eyes. "Wine-dark," Tyrone called her brown eyes.

But it was not of Tyrone, who had asked her to marry him, that Lauren wanted to think. It was of Eric, the sunburned playmate of all her yesteryears, to whom she had come to say good-bye.

Good-bye! There must be a better word. Good-bye was too sad—too abrupt and too final. There had been too many good-byes already. But this one was different—more literal and more heartbreaking in what should have been the happiest time of her 21 years. *This* parting meant that she and Eric had crossed childhood's borders forever, except for the memories. Most of them were wonderful, but one of them was too horrible to remember even now—the day that had taken away the sweet innocence of childhood and reshaped their hearts. She shivered and, trying to fold the corners of that long-ago revelation back into its burial place, tried to think only of today.

Today must be special. She must not think of its being an *Omega*, she thought with a smile, remembering what the Greek word had come to mean, but an *Alpha* in her life. After all, she reasoned, tomorrow she would be leaving her California home for Alaska. Yes, tomorrow the plane would take her to the "wildly beautiful frontier land," to visit her Aunt Nella, to work at a part-time job, and to concentrate on writing her first book. Most of all, she would allow herself enough time to sort out the flotsam of her heart.

Aunt Nella, her mother's only sister, disapproved of hasty decisions. Nella's invitation to head north was to give Lauren time "to get her head on straight." Timing was important, she said. Never having married herself, it was highly unthinkable that Lauren could consider marrying Tyrone, a "near-stranger." The fact that he was an engineer, unbelievably handsome in a dark, European way—the thin, aristocratic face marred only slightly by a little crook in the arch of his nose and a faint scar that traced the outline of his high cheekbone on the left side—had nothing to do with the decision.

Timing. At the thought of the word, Lauren unconsciously slowed her pace. Maybe Tyrone *had* been a little eager to claim her heart—and her lips. She remembered drawing back when he tried to embrace her and trying to explain that things in her world were different. There needed to be time before—well, intimacy.

"*Intimacy*? A harmless little kiss for the lady I plan to marry?" Tyrone said.

"*Marry*?" Even now Lauren's heart picked up speed. Why, he couldn't be proposing! They had met only two months earlier at a party where she had caused all eyebrows—including his—to raise in sophisticated amusement when she asked for "plain punch" at the social hour. With dark eyebrows still arched and a smile curving the thin but attractive lips, Tyrone had left the brittle-looking blonde girl beside him and made his way immediately to where Lauren stood.

How *could* this internationally sought-after man want to marry her so quickly? When she found the words to ask him, Ty was amused.

"Now, why *do* men propose?" And he had laughed at her question. The laugh sounded skilled, as if he had practiced a lot. Eric never laughed like that. Eric never laughed at all...

The crash of a wave breaking into foam along the shore brought Lauren back to the present. She began to run faster. "You're going to concentrate on today, remember?" she asked herself furiously.

Today...*today only*...

Then, suddenly out of the morning mist, Eric was there, jogging along beside her as he had for as long as either of them could recall. That's how it was with summer people who abandoned the city's noise and heat for the cool of the seashore. In the winters they forgot each other. Well, almost. Then, come summer, they resumed relationships as if there had been no time between—taking each other for granted, as if time stood still...

But Eric's presence was no invasion of privacy. She did not need to look up or to speak. She just knew that he was there. Eric was her other *self*.

"Finish school okay?" His voice was as powerful as Lauren remembered. Its deep gravel-tone gave strength to the gaunt, adolescently-thin frame. One would hardly take him for a lifeguard otherwise.

"So-so," she said of school. "I'm no whiz kid like you."

" 'For the wisdom of this world is foolishness with God.' "

"First Corinthians 3:19," Lauren, suddenly the partner of his childhood game, responded. "But you came in without knocking!"

"So I did." Eric's voice was barely audible above the complaints of the breakers as the rising tide hurled them against the jagged rocks near the cove. "The way we start our summers."

Yes...how true...Eric could open any door and enter abruptly, taking her with him wherever he chose to go. As they jogged on in silence, Lauren thought of their *knock-knock* game as being symbolic. It was just one of the many that his highly creative mind had improvised. And to her, his imaginative follower, all conventional games paled in comparison to his. He made her understand that the "Knock, knock, who's there?" twisting of words just "drained the brain of creative calories." "Games," he said, "should give the player something for storing up."

Oh, Eric-the-Wise, Eric-the-Wonderful! If he told her the man in the moon came tumbling down to ask for California Daylight Time, she would have believed him, and even have been grateful that he shared the information with an earthling like her. *The wizard of her youth...*

The heavy mists of the morning gave way to cloudlike wisps, resembling clouds come down to visit. Soon a breeze would part the light fog and before noon the warm sun would burn it off. But for now the two figures, a girl in blue shorts and shapeless white jersey, the boy looking all-of-a-single-color in suntan shorts that matched his bare chest and untamed hair, were alone in the mystic world. The slap-slap of their feet on the wet sand blended with the noisy screeching of dipping, darting gulls, hoarse warnings of a distant foghorn, and low, creaking groans of the jetties as they complained of the aches of another day.

This world was his—his and hers, because he had offered to share it. But soon the hordes of people would throng in, tearing apart the intimacy, as they always had in the past.

The girl broke the silence. "What would it have been like without—the others, Eric?" *In this case, our parents*, she might have added to somebody else. But with Eric, there was no need...

There had been no eye contact this morning, but Lauren felt the fierceness of his gaze. How earth-tone eyes could blaze like burning-out stars mystified her. How well she knew that look! It went with all the childhood-gone days when he said, "I, Eric-the-Wonderful, am about to make an announcement which can save mankind or destroy it."

Oh, wonderful world of fantasy! And today the familiar tingle of delicious awfulness rippled along her spine a she waited for Eric to answer.

"Maybe we'd have made it," he said slowly.

"To the stars?"

"And beyond."

"In your spaceship?"

"How else?"

"Eric—*would* you have taken me with you?"

"Of course. You wouldn't have been my sister—but for the *others*."

His sister. There, those words were out again. Well, what was she hoping for? That Eric, with all the knowledge—a student writing his doctoral dissertation in oceanography—had changed his stance? That he would say maybe they were wrong after all? And would she have accepted it if he had?

It would have been nice to share their burden long ago. Only nobody else would have understood. The others had never understood *anything* about "those strange children" of the past who had become "strange adults" of today. Their ideas. Their very conversations. Well, nobody else shared their Summer of Discovery...

Lauren, the "strange adult," squeezed her eyes shut and was Lauren, the "strange child." She was nine again. She saw herself coming down the beach, very much alone before the summer crowds. Her father, Cory Eldridge, a successful attorney, could vacation as he chose, and he liked to bring her and Roberta, her mother, early. That day it had been too early in the season to swim, so, wrapped in a warm beach towel, she stood glowering at the cold blue of the Pacific. Then it was cold no longer! Eric was there beside her without a greeting. Eric—my hero, her "summer," her *life*!

Eric's parents always came early too, because they

ran the inn. It was only natural that they should become best of friends with her own mother and father. Lauren's parents became "Uncle Cory" and "Aunt Berta" to Eric, just as the Thornes were "Aunt Erica" and "Uncle Fred" to her. It never occurred to the two children that their parents had a past—just a future. For her and Eric life began here every summer. And here it would continue until the space-ship was complete and the two of them left for other galaxies.

As she draped the oversized beach towel around her and padded along beside Eric that remembered morning, Lauren noticed that he was carrying an enormous war-surplus duffel bag. When she asked what it contained, Eric answered, "All the world's wisdom."

Even now Lauren recalled the tingling of her scalp. Eric's being three years older gave him a distinct edge on experience. He knew *everything*. How long it would take to get to the Milky Way and back—if they decided to return. How to survive on nectar from the evening-glories. (They were like morning-glories, only they bloomed at night when the stars were out, and their coils and runners held the points of the stars in place, Eric had said.) She had mastered the skill of sipping a droplet of nectar from the trumpet-shaped flowers they found along the beach—similar to the evening-glories of the Milky Way, Eric said. And she was striving to fence with the weapons he had whittled from driftwood in case of "attack." *Attack, Eric*? Of course, attack! By the giant sky squid that could squirt ink enough to drown this planet and all the others. *But there's no sea in the sky, Eric*. Then Eric had set her straight. What "the others" saw Up There was no sky at all. Up There all the seas were one sea in which the stars swam. Like the starfish swam in the sea Down Here. So what more could he tell her—except what was in the mysterious bag?

"Equipment for hacking off starfish in case we need more light. Already we have *Alpha* and *Omega*. We need *Beta, Andromeda,* and all the other stars in between—"

Lauren had been glad that she knew about their *Alpha* and *Omega*. On their first summer visit to The Little Church of the Sands, Eric had explained that they were the first and last letters of the Greek alphabet. When the scholarly-looking minister used the strange words (that she had supposed to be a language belonging to Eric which the rest of the world did not understand), Eric simply shrugged away the "coincidence." Then, unexpectedly, one day he added "Alpha and Omega" to their games.

"Whenever I say 'The Almighty,' can you tell me what you're supposed to say?" he asked on one of his Revelation Days.

She had thought hard. "*Eric*?" she guessed.

Eric looked as if she had struck him dead. "No!" he said darkly. "You say 'First'!"

"First," she repeated obediently.

"Then I say 'Last.' And you say 'Always.' *Then* we see who can say 'Revelation 1:8' first. Understand?"

Lauren hesitated. It was a complicated game.

"Lest the giant squid—" Eric's eyes burned into hers.

Lauren gulped. She *did* understand.

It would be nice to add a lot more star-names to

Alpha and *Omega*, Lauren had thought as they headed toward the cove the summer of her ninth birthday. "About the starfish—" she began.

But Eric put up a warning finger that fateful morning, the one she remembered so vividly—the repeating memory that came unbidden to haunt her dreams and remind her of its full interpretation. They were nearing the enchanted cave and there would be no more talk. Enemies could have invaded during the winter months while they were away. Spies might be everywhere—listening, wanting information about the spaceship he was building. It was all so real the way Eric explained it—more real than the world they were about to enter.

Lauren had shivered with apprehension as they slipped stealthily into the cool damp of the little cave, Eric's workshop. Then they stopped dead in their tracks. For there in the shadowy dark was a figure— no, two, a man and a woman, their bodies molded together as if they were one being. Somewhere above a tiny ray of sun crept through a crevice to illuminate the glory of her hair, outline the ivory sculpture of her face—its parted lips waiting surely for his kiss. *The others*!

"God never intended it to be like this, Erica," the man's husky voice, low and agonized, murmured against the sunlit hair.

The woman trembled. "I know, Cory, I know. And it's so unfair when Eric's not even *his*—and yet it's the children holding us apart."

But the children, *his* daughter and *her* son, heard no more. They were gone. White-faced, they raced against the salty spray, the rising tide washing away their footprints in the sand. That night Eric tore down the spaceship and hurled its pieces into the sea.

There was no longer a fear of the giant sky squid's ink. Their world had been destroyed before the creature could attack.

Farther than they had ever dared venture down the beach because of riptides, the two of them—lost and confused children—paused for breath. "We tell *nobody—nobody*," Eric near-sobbed, his face pale in spite of its tan.

Lauren's heart beat painfully against her small ribs. "Nobody," she whispered through frozen lips. "Not even *them*—that we know."

Eric spent the remainder of that summer formulating "rules." They had so many rules already. And there had to be a rule for this, he said. That the season was ruined made no difference to Lauren. She moved like a little-girl zombie in the faintly remembered world. The sky was no longer a turquoise sea of shining starfish, its tides rising and falling, waiting to be traversed. Food lost its taste. The world lost its beauty. And Lauren sensed no feeling except for a deep sense of grief that only abandoned children know. She had lost her parents. Eric had lost his. And, in some strange, unexplainable way, they had lost each other...

"A lot has happened since then," Eric resumed the conversation suddenly, bringing them back to the adult world.

Lauren inhaled deeply, trying to shake herself free of memories that hurt. "Yes," she said.

Yes, a lot had happened. The routine winters of feeling lonely in the crowd were followed by 11 golden summers on the beach, marred only by their Day of Discovery. Being an only child may have caused Lauren to miss Eric more during their time apart. Did he miss her as much? He was an only child too. Maybe loneliness could have brought them together. But, as the years went on, other ties held them together as she adjusted to braces and he adjusted to his new voice, pitched an octave lower. They swam. They surfed. They collected shells and they built castles in the sand. Odd, wasn't it, that they explored everything—except love? There was never so much as a first shy kiss to add to a summer's souvenirs. Well, not *really* odd, the way Eric explained it. "Siblings"—Eric knew such wonderful words!—did not kiss even when they were "half-brother-and-sister." Lauren never questioned. And, as the years tumbled by end-on-end, she came to accept the circumstances of their "kin" as she accepted all else that Eric said and believed. He was her wizard...

"That's where the freeway cuts through," Eric said suddenly now.

Lauren looked up to where he pointed at a long line of hungry-looking bulldozers lined above them on the cliff. Eric slowed his pace and she saw that they were nearing the cove. Gratefully she matched his gait..

"It's a shame," she said of the machinery.

"A shame," he repeated.

By unspoken agreement they stopped to look at the cliff about to be sacrificed. It was their private fairyland, an area that should be preserved. The two of them looked in near-reverence at the gnarled beauty of the Torrey Pines that reached from the red earth, permanently bent backward by the ocean breeze. Some seemed to grow out of bare rock. Others clung to crumbling dry soil. "Like people," Eric had said once. Destroying the eerie trees would be like taking human life. And yet it was mankind who was doing it.

"How could they do it? How *could* they?"

"I don't know. I—don't—know," Eric spaced his words almost angrily. "But, then," he inhaled deeply, "adults—the rest of them—are hard to understand."

"Doesn't anybody care? God meant those trees to be here."

"*One* cares. I'm working on it," Eric said quietly.

They turned to face each other, Eric's pale-eyes-turned dark and Lauren's brown ones wide-open with expectation. He did not disappoint her.

"If we could reserve that stretch of ancient pines, there could be more trails. People could come here in a wilderness kind of setting to write—draw—meditate. See that little cluster where the trees seem to form a dome?"

Yes, she saw.

"I can imagine that as a kind of chapel." His voice grew excited. "Couples could come here to exchange marriage vows—"

Oh, Eric, yes! But the moment was gone.

Eric dropped suddenly to the sand, doubling his long legs beneath him. When he patted a spot beside him, Lauren sat down obediently. The sun was breaking through the thinning fog, and already the sand felt familiarly warm to her bare thighs. She was going to miss this languid warmth up North. But, before Alaska, there were loose ends to tie up.

"Uncle Fred—how does he feel about the freeways taking the inn?" she asked of Eric's father.

"I don't know. He seldom lets go, you know."
Eric's voice was taut.

"Like Mother," she said softly.

"How *does* Aunt Berta feel about the cottage?"

"Relieved, I think." When Eric glanced up, Lauren
continued quickly, "I mean, she's not able to keep it
really—financially or physically either."

It was Eric's turn to agree. "Like Dad," he said.

"What about you, Eric? *How do you feel*?"

Deliberately, it seemed, he misunderstood the question. "I'll be away regardless—studying marine life.
Mexico first."

But summers? The Torrey Pines? She waited for
him to elaborate, but he asked instead, "And you?"

"I—I'm going away, too."

Away. I'm going away, Eric. Say something.

But there was silence except for the relentless moans
of the ocean over which Lauren imagined she could
hear the sighing of the pines above.

"We should be getting back. Aunt Berta likes lunch
on time." Eric rose and offered her a helping hand.
But, once both of them were standing, he hesitated
and studied some distant object at sea.

His question came as a total surprise. "Still keeping our sacred vows?"

The rules he had drafted over the years! Eric's
childhood "shalt nots" touched on everything from
strong drink to harming helpless animals. Then, on
the Day of Discovery, he had added the two that
neither of them had dared mention again, even to each
other: *Thou shalt not reveal sacred secrets. Thou shalt
not marry others*! The wording of the compact had
sounded sensible at the time of Eric's drafting it. He

had pierced each of their index fingers and they had made an *X*, first with the left hand and then with the right. It was their shed blood that made the rules in sacred vows, he had said.

Now Lauren searched the thin face for a smile, but there was none. Of course, Eric might laugh inside and there would be no trace of a smile on his craggy features. Even she could never tell.

Now was the time to say, "I've met a man, Eric. He's really quite wonderful, this man, and I can love him. We can make marriage work. We *can*!"

But Eric's moonstone eyes would bore into hers. "Then why are you so defensive?" he would demand.

"Because—" What *would* she say?

Eric was looking at her, waiting for her answer to his question about vow-keeping. "So far, yes," she answered truthfully if a little too quickly. "But—I— I'm going to Alaska," she finished lamely.

Lauren could feel his quizzical eyes on her face and felt hot color stain her cheeks. Deliberately she reached into the pocket of her jersey and took out her sunglasses. Fumbling to put them on, she said, "My aunt wants me to spend some time with her there— and Mother doesn't mind being alone. We're renting out a part of the house—easy to do in San Diego, you know. The heart condition is better—some ways."

Her dark glasses made it easier to tell him the rest: Aunt Nella's description of the Alaskan wilderness. Her job. The arrangements. But, under his probing gaze, she made no mention of the rest. She could tell him tomorrow that when she returned to stay, a year later, it would be to marry Tyrone Valdez.

Roberta Eldridge waved from a distance as Lauren

and Eric neared the cottage. Lauren felt her heart miss a beat and hated herself for it. She shouldn't feel so totally responsible for her mother's every motion and emotion, but she did, and today was no exception.

Eric seemed to sense danger too. Cupping his hands to his mouth, he called, "Coming—" But his voice was lost in the wind.

Then, suddenly, Lauren saw her mother hold her right fist to her ear and tilt her head as if listening. Of course, a telephone! Mother was signaling that someone was calling. She must hurry.

"See you tomorrow before I go," she called over her shoulder.

"Sure," Eric said. "Sure, I wouldn't want to miss that Eskimo kiss—they press their noses together, don't they?"

The light remark was out of character, but Lauren was preoccupied with rushing to pick up the telephone and did not think about it at the time.

Breathless from the run, she murmured a "Hello" into the mouthpiece.

A long distance operator said crisply, "Overseas call, miss. One moment please."

"Hel-*lo*!" Even with the hum of the distance between them, Tyrone's low-pitched, intimate voice was unmistakable.

Lauren concentrated on a pewter bowlful of oranges on the kitchen table. The bowl was one of the few things they had not packed yesterday in preparation for moving. Oranges, their color and smell, had always held a strange power over her. As a child she could scratch the peel of a tree-ripe orange and it became an Aladdin's lamp, a magic ring, or a flying carpet that transported her to another world. Maybe, if she concentrated hard enough, she could control the wild beating of her heart and steady her voice. Maybe she could float away.

But it was no use. "Ty—Ty—where are you?" she gasped.

"Paris, of course," he laughed from across the ocean. "But where are *you*?"

She raised her voice. "You weren't to contact me—"

"Your words, my love, not mine," he reminded her. "And the answer is yes?"

"I am no more prepared to answer than I was two weeks ago. You promised me time."

"But I didn't say how long. You love me. Now don't deny that!"

The pounding in her chest was suffocating. Lauren felt disorganized and disoriented and wished she were less hemmed in by "rules." If only she could let go the way other girls did, make snap decisions—even give in to a sensory delight they would feel at being kissed by telephone. And asked—no *urged*—to marry the rich and famous bachelor—

"Lauren?" Tyrone prompted. "What can matter if you love me?"

That you love me in return, Ty. Oh say it. Please say it!

"You're mine, you know," Tyrone's voice was low and compelling, and, while she thrilled to its possessiveness, she fet uneasy at being rushed. He was so attractive to other women, a friend had confided—as if that should make him the perfect mate. Instead, Lauren could not help wondering if this magnetic, wonderful man took it for granted that she too would—

A crackle of static broke into her thoughts. Ty was speaking, she realized, but his words were choppy. "...envelope...just stamp and mail...in Seattle?"

"I can't hear, Ty. Operator!"

"...change planes and...?"

"Change planes in Seattle? Is that what you need to know. Yes, yes, I do! But—"

"General Delivery...new envelope...drop in mail...there soon—"

Tyrone's voice faded away completely, and no amount of signaling could bring the operator on. When the dial tone told her the connection was broken, Lauren redialed, then hung up before the operator answered. How would she be able to call back when Ty had given no inkling of where he was staying? She had no idea what kind of project he was working on or where his work would take him. Actually, she thought, as her heart slowed down to normal, she knew little about him except that he was fascinating and wonderful, and that she was all but ready to accept his proposal of marriage.

Idly she reached for an orange, scraped its smooth peel with her thumbnail, and tried to put the meaningless scramble of words together. Obviously Ty knew that her plane would be landing in Seattle. But how did he know? She had no memory of telling him— not that it mattered. What else had he said?

Envelope. Then what? In Seattle she was to stamp and mail an envelope. A *new* envelope. General Delivery? No, that was how she would receive it, in all likelihood. But where? And what? The "there soon" must mean that the mysterious letter would be delivered sooner if she remailed it. It was baffling. Probably nothing she should worry about at all. Still, Lauren decided, it was a situation she did not wish to discuss with anyone else.

Over lunch, she and her mother talked of tomorrow's plans, reassuring each other that they would be all right.

"Alaska seems so—so *Arctic*!" Roberta said. "Are you really prepared?"

Lauren smiled at her mother. "I need the change, and a year's not forever. But prepared? Well, no, if you mean outfitted, it's summer there now."

"Aunt Nella will help you choose warm clothing."

"After I earn some money—not that the little newspaper can pay much. But I'll pick up some experience, and the hours will allow me time to work on the book. But you, Mother—are you sure you won't mind my going?"

"Of course I'll mind, kitten!" Roberta laughed. "But you will write and Uncle Fred will be close by. He plans to come down—"

When her voice trailed off, Lauren glanced furtively at her. Something in her mother's tone made her wonder for the first time just how much the two of them had leaned on each other when their mates betrayed them. She had always hoped that God in His mercy had spared them the truth. Maybe He had heard the fervent prayers that she and Eric used to send up from the secret crevice that only they and the tides knew about. They had never reentered their cave after discovering their other two parents there. But then had come the flaming crash that snuffed out the lives of

Lauren's father (and surely Eric's) and his mother. Lauren had said that maybe God couldn't hear their prayers above the breakers, but Eric said that God heard everything—"vibes" were different Up There—and, anyway, maybe He had decided to bury their secrets with them at sea.

Lauren shivered, remembering that the bodies of their parents were never recovered. That was seven years ago. Hopefully Eric was right.

"Are you all right?"

At her mother's question, Lauren jumped. "Oh, fine, just relaxed after the morning's workout. Want any more avocado?"

"You finish the salad. You'll miss the avocadoes—and the oranges."

"I will. But, like I said, it won't be forever."

Lauren finished the salad and was about to pick up the remnants of the sandwiches when her mother put a detaining hand on her arm. "Lauren," she said tentatively, "is—is there anything you would like to discuss?"

"No!"

Too late she realized that the word was too sudden and too abrupt. Worse, the tone was not lost to her mother's ears.

"I know you were always upset about the accident—"

"Please, Mother," she whispered.

"All right, but if you ever do—darling, you would ask—"

I don't need to ask! I know, Mother. I know and I pray that you never do! Aloud, she answered, "Yes, if ever."

"I'm glad you and Eric have remained friends."

Lauren tried to stretch her tight lips into a smile. "Friends, yes. Are you finished with the melon?"

Roberta Eldridge gave an unexpected little sigh. "I wish—never mind what I wish. But I did want to ask you something. Have I your permission?"

Lauren picked up the salad plates and turned her back. "Of course," she said with a calm she did not feel.

"Well, I did not intend to eavesdrop, but I overheard part of your conversation on the phone. Is this a new friend?"

Lauren sucked in her breath. She hadn't wanted to discuss Tyrone with her mother until she talked with Eric, but she disliked being evasive. "Fairly new. But more than a friend in a way—would you mind terribly if we leave it there for now? I'll tell you if anything definite comes of it."

"It's just that you've never cared much for the company of men—except for Eric. And you sounded almost—shall I say reluctant?"

"I *am* reluctant, Mother. Reluctant to discuss it right now, that is." She hoped that the tone of finality would end the conversation.

And it did except for her mother's small, almost inaudible remark. "Just don't let yourself be rushed. And make sure the love is mutual."

Sleep was slow in coming that night. And, once asleep, Lauren was haunted by senseless dreams in which she and her mother kept falling in love with the wrong men. When the foghorn awoke her before dawn, Lauren crept into the little living room. Her plane would leave Lindbergh Field at ten, so she might as well stay up. Eric might come for breakfast. In fact, it would be nice if he and Uncle Fred joined her and Mother for blueberry muffins. She would call and see.

But when she dialed, there was no answer. But of course! It was early. Both men were probably asleep, and she should not have disturbed them. Maybe she would jog early. She opened the door to test the temperature and found a little note: *"Knock, knock... 'The Almighty'!"*

The old bitterness swept over Lauren, followed by the familiar sadness. This summer had ended without having started at all. Only *she* would know that the message meant good-bye. That's the way it always was. Eric's idea of the perfect farewell was to start a game and leave it unfinished. "Then see who can remember where we left off!" he challenged—when they met again. *If* they met again...

But why didn't he tell her he was leaving today for Mexico? Why did he let her take it for granted that she knew he would no longer be watching out for the safety of guests who ignored rules and had to be pulled from the undercurrents? Sadness gave way to anger—anger at Eric for not telling her, then anger at herself for not asking. But the anger passed and the empty-inside feeling came back.

Fighting tears, Lauren wadded the note into a tight little ball. Then, carefully—as if it were a sacred document—she smoothed it out on her knee to be filed away with the rest of her summer souvenirs.

Chapter Two

Lauren leaned to look out the window, glad that the morning fog had lifted and she could have one last view of "home" as the 747 zoomed into the sky. She could almost feel the warm breeze of the beach below. It always came in little puffs, as if it had been running as it moved among the palms, causing the trees to fan themselves, sigh, and settle back to silence as the wind went back to the sand.

In that timeless silver-blue moment, it came as no surprise to Lauren that a couple strolled in the early-morning still. She and Eric belonged there—permanently, like the dunes held in place by little tufts of grass. But a capital "V" of birds, flapping silent wings, then sailing, blocked the strollers from her view. Birds, like summer, seemed to have no purpose except to practice formation flying.

The big jet tilted a wing, allowing one last look at the Torrey Pines and a little field of poppies where she and Eric had picnicked so often. When the plane righted itself, Lauren leaned back and tried to concentrate on the great adventure that lay ahead.

Lauren had wished she knew her geography better when Aunt Nella spoke of the little settlement's being "up the Yukon." Try as she would, she was unable to locate anything sounding like *Kakalota* on the map. Probably too small. The population was less than 200, her aunt had written. "And, while city folks in Alaska may never have seen a polar bear outside a zoo, it's not that way here. It's primitive, *very* primitive, which is why you'll love it! No dogsleds, but no parking meters for the snowmobiles either! We do have furnaces, but no air conditioning. And as for the founding of the little newspaper—well, why don't I just let you find out some of these things for yourself?"

When Aunt Nella promised to have a private plane to meet her, Lauren reflected that her mother's sister must be better off financially than she had suspected. It was just another of the countless mysteries, the first of which she must face in Seattle.

And Seattle was closer than Lauren realized. One moment the plane was cruising above forests that stretched into eternity. The next moment it was nosing downward with the FASTEN SEAT BELTS light on.

As soon as the plane rolled to a stop she collected her belongings quickly and hurried to the exit.

"Where is the information desk?" Lauren asked the stewardess.

"Straight ahead," the girl smiled.

Lauren murmured a thank you and walked briskly forward. As she recalled, there was less than half an hour before her connecting flight to Fairbanks.

There was nothing for her at the infromation desk, a polite clerk told her. And, no, there was no sub-station nearby. He gave directions to the main post office, then consulted his watch. "Better call a cab," he advised.

Lauren checked her camera, makeup kit, and book manuscript. Then, with the strap of her travel bag swung over her right shoulder, she signaled a cab and asked the driver to take her to the main post office.

"Yes," the uncompromising window clerk said, "there is a letter for a Ms. Lauren Eldridge, but—" and, adjusting tinted glasses which made eye contact impossible, he murmured something and moved away.

The next few minutes were exasperating. The letter was registered, the clerk said upon his return. Lauren would have to sign for it. But first did she have any identification—preferably a passport? No passport, she explained hurriedly, but she was American, she blurted, wondering if he would demand proof. Her credit cards and driver's license would suffice, the man said, after he had examined the cards for what seemed like a quarter-hour. Maybe she only imagined that he looked at her oddly.

When at length she was allowed to sign, Lauren almost snatched the envelope in her haste, ripped it open, and would have deposited the inside envelope in the slot immediately. But it bore no stamp.

"Next, please!" the clerk called over her head.

"No, wait—please, I need a 20-cent stamp—and I'm in such a rush—"

The man inhaled tiredly. "Better register it," he said tonelessly.

Well, of course! But that took more time. She counted out the fee so there would be no need for change. "And you'll need to sign this." He shoved a card across the counter.

"*And*," as if in a delay tactic, "put a return address on the outside."

Lauren was near tears by the time she located Aunt Nella's address at the bottom of her bag, scribbled it in the proper place, and deposited the envelope. She scrambled out of the building and saw that the driver had waited. Breathlessly, she boarded the plane just before the doors were closed. Only then did it occur to her that she had no idea to whom the letter she had mailed would go. For some reason, the thought made her uneasy.

In Fairbanks, Lauren was paged. A dark-skinned young man wearing goggles and a Lindbergh-era helmet gave her a scrutinizing look. "You Miz Eldridge?" When she nodded, he pointed to a small plane with flaking camouflage paint. She followed him to the runway.

"Are you in Miss Trusdale's employ?" she asked curiously.

"I work fer all Kakalota," he answered. Even above the hum of the warming engine Lauren recognized a Southern drawl. She could imagine Eric's explanation. "A Southern Eskimo," he would say without a smile.

The countryside over which they flew was refreshingly green but sparsely populated, Lauren noted. She wondered how the pilot had enough business to make a living. As they wound along the twisting river, the houses seemed to disappear altogether in the vastness of the forests—which reminded her that it should be dark! Back in Fairbanks she had noticed that the hands on the wall clock were at 10 P.M., but the sun was still shining below them! What a strange country!

Without warning the little plane dipped down with a jolt. For a terrifying moment Lauren thought they might have crashed. Then they were bumping down a narrow runway.

"Somebody gonna pick you up?" the pilot asked as he lifted Lauren's baggage from the plane.

"Why, I—I just supposed this would be it. The town, I mean."

The young man grinned. "Kakalota's no town, strictly speakin'. A village, settlers like sayin'. But she's less'n that, really. As fer how you get there—"

But even as he spoke there was a buzz that became the deep-throated roar of a car, truck, or some other vehicle. An olive-drab jeep parted the brush and Aunt Nella, wearing blue jeans and a Western hat, jumped from behind the steering wheel and rushed forward. "It's good to see you, baby!" Her aunt gave her a tight squeeze and said to the pilot, "Thanks, Hank. Doc'll be needing you the day after tomorrow."

As the jeep groaned over the narrow mountain road, Lauren had a chance to review her aunt's face. "Do I look the same?" Nella surprised her by asking. "The years are tattletales," she laughed.

"Exactly," Lauren laughed back. And it was true. Her aunt was anything but beautiful, but she had the kind of good bone structure that made beauty seem unimportant. And her eyes, though pale, were always merry. The freckles, characteristic of the Trusdale women and an embarrassment to Mother, never seemed to trouble her older sister.

"Well *you* don't look the same! But of course you're grown up. How long has it been?"

"Five years—and fours years before that. You came for the—"

"Memorial service," Nella said practically, then concentrated on her driving. Lauren's stomach began to feel queasy. It had been a long, unsettling day. Being bounced about and choked by dust did not help the situation. Lauren was about to ask if they could stop when the older woman announced, "The commune's just around the bend."

"Commune?"

Nella laughed. "That's what I call it, though goodness knows the friar has tried to joke me out of it. He likes to call it an inn, and in the summer it is, sort of. We have guests there now. But in winter— well, it becomes a commune again. Safety-in-numbers kind of thing. But, then, you don't know about Alaskan winters."

Lauren wiped dust from her eyes as best she could before answering. "I'm going to like the summers. The long daylight's wonderful. Doesn't the sun ever set?"

Nella laughed again. "Wait, just you wait. Sooner than you think you'll be asking doesn't it ever rise!"

The jeep came to a sudden halt. Lauren gulped and tried to swallow. There were guests, Aunt Nella said, and being sick would be embarrassing, to say the least. She tried to look around as the two of them unloaded her luggage. Surely the nausea would pass.

The building was low, rambling, and wide-eaved. The outside had a certain character, as if the heavy timbers had withstood many a storm and had no intention of retiring. But the architecture! The rooms (and there were lots of them) seemed to be separate entities, and yet each joined the others by means of little runways. The result was an enormous horseshoe-shaped structure. The doors were massive, and the few windows seemed to peer through the blossoming foliage of the vines which arched above them like quizzical eyebrows.

"You *live* here?"

Nella nodded. "Along with the others. You'll meet them shortly."

"But the doctor you spoke of—he lives in the village?"

"He lives here."

Lauren was almost afraid to ask her next question. "The newspaper—where will it be published?"

"Here, too. Such as it will be. I'll let Doc and the friar tell you the details. It's more of a newsletter, actually—you know, information, instructions, and the like for the patients and the parishioners."

"And you—"

Lauren could feel her aunt studying her face. "I am owner, official hostess, manager, and morale-booster. Now, no more questions until you've met the family you're getting into!"

"May I help?" a warm, friendly voice asked at Lauren's elbow.

"Oh," Nella looked up from the bags. "Lauren, this is Dr. Piriot. My niece, Doc—Lauren Eldridge from San Diego."

"Miss Eldridge," the short, somewhat stout man (about 40 years old, Lauren guessed) acknowledged the introduction politely. What was the accent? French, maybe. "Are you all right?" he asked with professional concern.

"I'm fine, thank you. Just a little weary."

"Be cautious here. The climate can be deceptive." With surprising strength, Dr. Piriot lifted the bags and led the way into an enormous roomful of couches, easy chairs, and animal-skin rugs. Lauren's eyes noted with appreciation the collections of Indian artifacts and impressionistic paintings which lined the walls beside the wide-mouthed native-rock fireplace. Comfortable. Livable. Perfect for reading, she thought. Another turn of her head revealed one entire wall lined with books. "Our all-purpose room," Nella said smilingly.

"Boss la--dee!"

The high-pitched voice came from a door which led, Lauren was to learn later, to the dining room. Nella, who must be "Boss Lady," responded immediately. "Yes, Tuk?"

"How mean-ee?" The woman smiled broadly to reveal white, square teeth.

Nella responded by using her finger as an abacus. "This is Miss Eldridge, Tuk," and to Lauren, "Tuk's our cook." Then she went back to her counting. "Doc, the friar, Jessica, and the Petrovs. Eight counting you," Nella pointed to the still-smiling cook and then to herself, "and me. Eight, Tuk. See?" She held up eight fingers.

Tuk's almond-shaped eyes danced. "A-eight!" she giggled. Then the low, square figure waddled back into the shadows from which she had emerged. "Eskimo?" Lauren whispered. Nella nodded in reply.

The doctor, who had deposited the bags and waited until Nella and Tuk finished talking, tapped Lauren lightly on the shoulder. "Miss Eldridge?"

"Lauren, please."

Dr. Piriot nodded. "Lauren, may I present Father Troy?"

Troy Huguenot was a tall man, dark-haired, with a very lean, aesthetic face. There was something akin to compassion and understanding in his brown eyes. Aunt Nella was to explain later that these were the essential characteristics of a priest (she addressed him teasingly as the friar) who had to minister to a diverse culture of parishioners, many of whom were decidedly less than pious.

"Welcome, Miss Eldridge. You are sorely needed here."

His words and manner surprised Lauren. Just how she could be needed was still a question, but the idea—spoken so gently and quietly in a strongly accented voice—pleased her. Maybe there *was* purpose here.

But not as far as Jessica was concerned! Jessica Dunaway, Dr. Piriot's niece and nurse as well, was the next occupant that Lauren was to meet. It was obvious immediately that Jessica saw her as competition. But over what or whom? It could hardly have to do with a job and, as far as she could tell, there wasn't an eligible male at the inn. Even if there had been, Lauren's sun-and-salt naturalness could hold no threat to this willowy beauty with a cloud of black hair. But Jessica's steel-blue eyes were honed to fine points as they appraised her.

"I hope we'll be friends," Lauren managed when Troy Huguenot introduced the other girl.

"Let's," Jessica said breezily. But there was

no hint of friendliness in her voice.

"Now," Nella turned to Lauren. "Let's get you settled. You've met the family, such as we are, except for the guests, Anna and Ivan."

Lauren picked up her purse. "I'll bring your cosmetic kit. One of the men will bring along the bags. We all pitch in and help. It's just a fact of life."

And I like it that way, her aunt's tone of voice said. Lauren was beginning to think that she would like it too.

Her queasiness had given way to a new feeling of excitement and a certain languor that felt almost euphoric. The fact that she had had so little rest and food seemingly had not taken its toll. She no longer felt tired as Nella led her through door after door that let them pass through a countless number of halls.

"Yours," her aunt said, stopping at what must be the very last of the long chain. It was all so new, so exciting, but awesome, too.

Lauren was relieved when Nella said, "And I'm right next door."

When the older woman would have turned to go, Lauren detained her with a touch on her work-reddened hand. "Aunt Nella—"

"Can't we dispense with formalities? You're grown up now, so let's drop the title. Mind?"

"I'd like that. It does away with the genera-tion gap." At her aunt's nod of approval, Lauren continued, "Nella, why does Jessica dislike me?"

Nella appeared to consider, and when she spoke it was to say slowly, "It isn't that she dislikes you—not you personally."

"Then why did she give me such strange looks."

Nella laughed. "It's what you stand for. Being a young lady—"

A knock interrupted and Troy Huguenot's soft, well-modulated voice announced that Lauren's bags were at her "disposal." Lauren opened the heavy door, and when she thanked him he murmured something in French and walked away quietly. Such a nice, straight physique.

Nella smiled as Lauren closed the door and looked for a change of clothes. "That!" she said. "*That* is Jessica's objection to your presence. The warm look of appraisal you gave him."

"Father Troy! But he's a *priest*—the idea is preposterous."

"Not really. He's of the Protestant faith, educated in a kind of brotherhood seminary but not bound by vows of celibacy."

"But obviously his lifework means more to him than a private life."

Nella shook her head. "Not necessarily. He came here penniless, hardly able to speak English but knowing how to communicate with the French, Indian, and Eskimo peoples alike. It's not just a matter of language, you know? It's sort of a language of the soul."

Lauren was beginning to understand. "He's French?"

"French descent," Nella corrected. "Actually, he came—or was driven, as the story goes—from Russia. Strangely enough, though, neither ancestry nor place of residence has aroused the village people's natural suspicions of a foreigner. He finds a way to communicate with every family. He needs help with

English, admittedly, and that's where you come in. He knows about your background with writing."

"But Jessica—?"

"—thinks it's time he was marrying," Nella finished.

"And has the mate chosen," Lauren said with amusement.

"Of course! Then you had to show up and spoil the plans."

"But I'm no competition," Lauren felt her cheeks grow warm. "I'm—"

"You asked for a reason," Nella reminded her and turned toward the door. There she paused to say before leaving, "Incidentally, we 'dress' for dinner here, if you can imagine! Sort of keeps us civilized. Wear something simple. Oh, and the bath's at the end of the hall."

"Bath? *Singular*?"

"Bath singular—at least on this wing. The men share on the other end of the ell. And this is modern— wait till you see the village!"

Dinner was pleasant, with most of those around the table teasing Lauren, the newcomer, as a "tenderfoot." Dr. Piriot asked if he might serve her "baked Alaska," then carved a generous slice of salmon from the whole fish which centered the long, picnic-style table. Father Troy (as all but Nella addressed him) made a mock apology about being sorry they were out of blubber, "A delicacy you would relish!"

Jessica smiled at the banter. At least her *lips* smiled, but her eyes did not reflect the smile. When Father Troy said with appreciation, "You look lovely, Miss Eldridge," Lauren caught a look in the other girl's eyes which startled her. It was almost animalish in its possessiveness.

Uncomfortable, Lauren made a point of saying in a little aside, "Your gown is charming, Jessica." The dress *was* beautiful, she thought, if a trifle revealing—maybe chosen with a purpose for the evening. If so, Lauren was sure she was no competition. She had chosen a simple, long A-line skirt, with a wide black belt separating the floral material from a white peasant blouse.

"Thank you," Jessica said briefly, then turned to talk with her uncle about a patient in the village.

The newlyweds, Anna and Ivan Petrov, acknowledged their introduction to Lauren and then carried on a little tete-a-tete all their own. The other diners simply did not exist. Natural for honeymooners, Nella said later, but Lauren wondered. While neither of them addressed her directly, several times she felt their eyes turning in her direction. Curiosity? Or was it something more?

Anna was lovely in a silvery sort of way. Her hair was so blonde that it was almost white as it glistened beneath the wagon wheel of lights above the dining table. There was an aura of moonlight about Anna, Lauren thought, in direct contrast to her husband's dark almost-sullen handsomeness. Something about Anna's severely tailored dinner dress said "designer label." Her understated elegance and Ivan's almost contemptuous eyes—except when they were on his wife—made Lauren wonder about the couple's identity. But nobody else showed any attention, let alone concern, so she dismissed the Petrovs from her mind and enjoyed the after-dinner coffee.

It would have been nice to walk after the big meal. Lauren knew, however, that she needed rest. Nella, being the minder she was, eyed her sharply. "To bed with you, young lady!"

"No need to vote on it," Lauren assented, and after good nights, she followed her aunt down the long ell again.

As she brushed her hair, Lauren tried to reconstruct the day in her mind. But bits and pieces, like fragments of colored glass in a kaleidoscope, kept shifting positions each time they achieved a near-symmetrical design. Scenes of sand, pine, and poppies gave way to dark forests, snow-packed mountains, and desolation. Then, out of the chaos, came a strange pattern which blended them all together beautifully—and then fell to nothingness.

When Eric's face, serious as always, flashed before her, Lauren decided it must be fatigue. But when the pattern changed and Tyrone's magnetic eyes replaced Eric's face, Lauren laid down her hairbrush in near-panic. Irrationally, she thought that the two men should leave her alone. Neither of them had any right to intrude on her privacy.

Determinedly picking up the brush, Lauren began to count the strokes like she had as a child. Then, on the count of 46, Troy Huguenot's voice seemed to be counting with her—the quiet, gentle accent a sort of lullaby to her tired senses.

No, no! This was dangerous, letting herself be lulled into a false security. She had come here to put her life into its proper perspective—not to run away from it. And certainly not to complicate it!

Lauren felt a moment's temptation to put on her

robe and run to her mother's sister, as she had done the night after her father's memorial service. The two of them had prayed quietly and she had gone to sleep in her aunt's arms.

But now as she reached for her robe, Lauren decided to pray alone. Snapping off the light, she dropped to her knees. In the quiet semidarkness Lauren thought she heard the sound of quiet footsteps outside her door. Nella? She listened, but the sound was not repeated. Her imagination, most likely. She prayed then—haltingly at first, and then the words came easily. At last the tears came—tears she had held for so long. Surely she was drenching the sheets and the light blanket that Nella had laid out thoughtfully at the foot of the bed.

Finally she was exhausted. Climbing into bed, she fell into deep, dreamless sleep.

Chapter Three

She *did* hear footsteps! Lauren sat straight up in bed, her heart thumping crazily. Was it morning or had darkness failed to come at all? As she pulled a corner of the drape open to let in a stream of sunlight, there was a soft knock at the door.

"Lauren?" Nella inquired softly.

Feeling foolish at her fears, Lauren jumped out of bed and released the night latch. "Good morning! Have I overslept?"

"It wouldn't have mattered. Breakfast is anytime. We only get together evenings."

Yesterday's fatigue and last night's hallucinations were gone. Lauren felt refreshed and wonderful. "I'm glad you called. I don't want to miss a minute of this."

"There's plenty of time," Nella said with her usual don't-rush-into-things caution. "I wouldn't have called you except that Doc insisted on showing you around."

"Great! I'm anxious to get started."

"You were going to rest and write first—"

"I *am* rested. And the writing's what I'm here for."

"I meant your book."

"Oh, I take it with me—the questionnaires—"

Was it amusement that Lauren saw in Nella's gray eyes? But before she could decide what was amusing, her aunt was speaking again.

"Doc's going up to the village and insists you're to go along."

Lauren reached for a clean pair of pants and a lightweight sweater top. "These okay?" At Nella's nod, she asked, "And you did say *up?*"

"Yes, Kakalota's quite some distance up the mountain. Doc will take one of the jeeps. Troy has the other one. He teaches at the mission two days a week. Tomorrow he'll make house calls."

"Is Jessica going with her uncle and me?" Lauren cinched up her belt, checked her handbag, and picked up a pen and clipboard.

Nella laughed. "She's with Troy! Probably set her alarm and was waiting for him in the jeep—although she usually assists Doc. He won't be doctoring today, just *indoctrinating*—not that she'd have changed her plans!"

Dr. Piriot was waiting in the hall. He exchanged polite greetings with Lauren and then asked, "Are you sure you feel like the trip?"

"I feel fine. I'll feel even finer after coffee."

"*And* a good breakfast." His voice was a quiet order. "We have a hard climb ahead."

When they waved good-bye to Nella, Lauren thought she detected a small look of envy in her aunt's eyes. She wondered for the first time if Dr. Piriot had a wife.

At first there were a few trees along the mountainside, but after a hairpin turn they disappeared as the little jeep crawled upward. The road was frighteningly narrow, causing Lauren to wonder if the vehicle had good brakes. Once she dared ask, "Is there room for two cars in case we meet somebody?"

Dr. Piriot kept his eyes expertly on the road. "There is no danger, my dear," he assured her kindly. "Nobody uses the road except those of us from the inn, and we sign in and out just for precaution. Father Troy and Jessica are well ahead."

Lauren caught her breath as the doctor changed gears. She exhaled only when the low growl of the motor assured her that the gear was holding. Then the jeep began to climb what seemed to be a flat wall. Lauren pulled the extra sweater she had brought along around her, wondering if the temperature was changing or whether her chill came from downright fear.

When at last they stopped, Dr. Piriot handed Lauren a windbreaker. "Put it on," he cautioned. "It's colder here. Glacier country."

Gratefully she zipped up the lined jacket. Her clothes were all wrong. And shopping wasn't the easy matter she had supposed.

For the first time, Lauren looked at their surroundings. Snowy peaks towered above the wide plateau they had reached. And small wonder she was shivering! A wide sheet of snow, mixed with rocks and large masses of earth, spread down into the little cluster of crude buildings. What an unlikely building spot!

"What—what would happen if that thing moved?"

"The ice mass? Oh, it does—several feet a day."

Lauren gasped at the words and hoped fervently that they would get whatever they came for over with shortly. Too late, she realized that she had missed some of the doctor's words.

"—some of the country still unexplored on up from here. They do come down, a few of them, but some of the others have never seen white people."

The Eskimos, she supposed he meant. "That's why we need to get information to them—you know, safety rules, offer of help, that kind of thing."

"But if they can't read—"

"Some of the children are beginning to recognize words, and with the aid of some drawings—Can you draw?"

"Crudely," she admitted.

"Come with me. I'll show you around. See, there's the mission." He pointed to a small hut-shaped building alongside what must be the jeep that Troy had driven up the mountain.

The "village" was an eye-filling spectacle. Lauren swallowed to keep from bursting into tears as she and Dr. Piriot advanced toward a crudely printed sign saying TRADEPOST. Never in her wildest imaginings could she have envisioned such primitive conditions. No wonder her aunt had looked at her with amusement! How preposterous that she would have thought of gathering information for a book on marriage *here!*

At the door of the box-shaped, windowless trading post, Dr. Piriot stopped to say, "Don't expect much, Miss—"

"Lauren. And there is no need to explain. I— uh, wondered where the igloos are," she said, hoping to sound lighter-hearted than she felt.

"Farther east, although most are not made entirely of ice, as you might have thought." She had never thought much about it. There was no need to in California. *Eric,* she thought, *you are seeing the other side of the world...there will be so much to say next summer...only there isn't going to be a next summer for us....*

Determinedly pushing thoughts of the past as far into the bottom of her heart as she could reach, Lauren followed Dr. Piriot's gaze to the ragged little houses with their peculiar rounded roofs. She supposed the purpose of their shapes was to shed as much of the winter snow as possible. Other than a wisp of thin smoke coming from some of the small buildings, there was no sign of life anywhere.

It was almost a relief when they walked into the dank darkness of the post. After her eyes adjusted to the lack of light, Lauren saw the walls were lined with furs, Indian blankets, a few woven baskets, dried fish (strung like ornamental peppers), and several crude attempts at artwork from which the paint was peeling. A man—Indian, she imagined—sat on a stool, his face almost hidden by an ancient felt hat below which fell a long braid of black hair.

"Hello, Charlie."

The man did not look up at the doctor's greeting. He simply grunted.

Totally out of keeping was the table of brightly labeled canned goods in the center of the room. Dr. Piriot picked up several cans and paid the proprietor, who then broke his silence with a rush of jargon. Apparently her companion understood that the man wanted more money.

"What language was that?" Lauren asked curiously once they were outside again.

"A mixture of everything," he explained. "You may have guessed that we donate a lot of these things and then buy them back again."

The other jeep was gone when they returned to the parking spot. Then they began the long descent in low gear. Lauren lost herself in thought.

★　★　★

At dinner Troy addressed Lauren directly: "Would you wish to be *my* guest tomorrow?"

"Of course!" she responded immediately. After all, this was a part of her job.

But her quick response must have communicated overeagerness to Jessica. "I'll come along," she said warmly. "Lauren might appreciate a woman's view." Her eyes, however, were on Father Troy.

"You are to remain here!" Dr. Piriot's voice was almost sharp. "I will be needing you. Hank's to take us downriver to check on the accident victims." His niece made no reply.

"Like the biscuits?" Nella directed the question to Lauren, and she was relieved at the shift in the conversation.

"Love them. Yeast?"

To her surprise, those at the table laughed. "We're all supposed to know these are sourdough," Anna Petrov said with a faint smile. It was the first time Lauren had heard the girl speak, and the rather harsh accent surprised her. She had expected a music-box voice, in keeping with Anna's petite, blonde beauty.

Again, she wondered about the couple. What could they be doing in this isolated spot instead of at one of the many inviting places in the state on a honeymoon? What *is* the matter with me? she wondered. She had been seeing too many suspense movies. Next she'd be suspecting defectors or spies! It was good that she was well away from television....

Lauren turned back to the conversation. Her aunt and the doctor were discussing "starters" for sourdough and gently challenging one another to a bake-off. "You will have no lack of volunteer judges, I assure you," Father Troy assured them.

After coffee and a steamed pudding dessert, Nella asked the group to excuse her and Lauren. "We have had no time to catch up on the news at all," she explained.

Father Troy rose and said formally, "Good night, Miss Eld—Lauren."

Lauren felt rather than saw Jessica's eyes on her. Undoubtedly, her sharp ears had picked up the man's use of her first name. "Good night, Father Troy," Lauren said, making her voice as demure as possible. If only, she thought, I can make her understand that I have no designs on him—that I do not need a third man to mess up my life!

"Tomorrow morning?" Father Troy reminded.

"I'm looking forward!" Lauren said, and could have bitten her tongue. She had spoken with more warmth than a polite response demanded, and she saw his quick glance of interest. Now she had misled them both!

"I have a way of saying all the wrong things with everybody," Lauren said to her aunt as they walked through the halls to their rooms.

"Forget it," Nella advised, unlocking the door to her bedroom.

Lauren looked around with appreciation. The room was like her own—comfortable, with the necessary bed, desk, and chests. Nella had had an opportunity to make her quarters more inviting with scatter rugs, hangings, and bouquets of dried flowers.

"Take off your shoes and get comfy," the older woman said.

When Lauren was settled, she smiled at her aunt. "Now, ask away!"

"First, Roberta. How is she?"

Lauren filled her in on her mother's plans, to which Nella nodded as if in approval. "It will do her good to be alone."

"No!" Lauren objected quickly. "Mother has always needed me."

Nella bit her lip in concentration. "Less than you thought, baby. Now don't be hurt by that! She needed your love—there's never enough of that, goodness knows. But not necessarily your—how shall I say it— your physical presence? Your protection?"

Sadness swept over Lauren, a sadness which must have reflected in her face. "You don't understand."

Nella inhaled deeply. "Could it be that it's *you* who doesn't understand? How much has she told you?"

"Mother? Why, there's nothing to tell. It's the other way around!" Too late she realized that she had blurted the words out—

But if her aunt noticed, she gave no indication. Instead, she said something that Lauren was to puzzle over in the days to come. "She *hasn't* told you. But enough on the matter for now. Let's talk about your young man.''

Her "young man" didn't fit Tyrone somehow. The words spawned images of a childhood sweetheart or a clean-shaven undergrad in loafers—not Ty with his lean, perfect body molded into a carelessly-expensive suit...Ty with his mysterious eyes probing Lauren's beneath his dark, arched brows...Ty hurrying to catch a plane, an attache case swinging in perfect cadence with his swinging gait...Ty with his sensitive hands reaching out in a ready-to-caress manner, the gold signet ring always evident. The signet ring! Strange that she would remember the ring...

"Lauren?" Nella prompted.

"I'm sorry," Lauren murmured in confusion. "It's just that—when you're in love—"

"You *are* in love, then?" Nella probed gently.

Lauren's head jerked up. "Whatever gave you the impression that—well, of course I am!" Too late she realized that the words sounded defiant.

"The once-in-a-lifetime way? The kind that will last and not end up—well, you know how."

"I know very well," Lauren said in a small voice. "But it's time I made a decision what to do with my life. I want to have a family—love and be loved—"

"And does he love you the same way?"

Oh, Aunt Nella, the voice of her childhood cried out, *I don't know how I love Ty, how he loves me, or whether he really loves me...*

Eric wouldn't have understood. Neither would Mother. But she had a feeling that Nella and she could talk. And they would. But not now.

Chapter Four

Father Troy's eyes met Lauren's eyes as she entered the dining room. His face seemed to come alive with a little smile of appreciation of her blue pants suit and the pink sweater top. "We're very early and that will be nice," he said. The others apparently were not up or had gone their separate ways. There was a little air of intimacy as they drank the deep-amber coffee. Although their being alone was unplanned, Lauren decided to take care to avoid situations which might arouse more suspicion in Jessica than was there already—and situations which might be misleading to this gentle, unassuming man.

Father Troy cleared his throat, and guiltily Lauren realized that he had asked her a question. "I'm sorry," she laughed. "I—I was halfway up the mountain with my thoughts, I guess."

When he looked at her solemnly, Lauren realized that she may have again said something differently than she had intended. Flustered, she said, "I missed what you were saying."

"That you must eat a better breakfast."

"Usually a butterhorn's enough—or cold cereal."

"May I recommend the pancakes? They're sourdough." And, without waiting for a reply, he laid four of the golden-edged, yeasty-smelling rounds on her plate.

"Wow!" She groaned with a smile. "Want me to be too heavy for a dogsled when I leave here?"

"You're too fragile, my dear—far too fragile for the winters. And we will worry about how to transport you when the time comes." He lifted the lid from the butter dish, and for an amusing moment she thought he was going to butter the pancakes for her. Instead, he handed the dish to her and continued. "You may decide to remain here, you know. I must caution you that there's a strange sort of beauty here that gets into the blood."

"I know," she said. "I can feel it already."

Immediately Lauren regretted those words. She was sure that they were responsible for the way Father Troy's hand lingered on hers for a bit longer than was necessary as he handed her the pitcher of warmed syrup.

Embarrassed, she wolfed down the pancakes with what he mistook for appetite. "Excellent!" he applauded. "We can be on our way now."

Driving took all of Father Troy's attention. Lauren noted with relief that the trip seemed a little less perilous on the second trip up.

First they would visit the mission, he told her after he had parked the jeep. "Is school in session?" she asked.

"To a degree, yes. One of the women here helps in my absence, although she is able to manage very little English."

Inside, Lauren was aware of about a dozen pairs of round, dark eyes focused on her face. At first the children looked fearful. But after their obviously adored "Master" introduced her as "Teacher," fear gave way to curiosity.

Smiling broadly, one little girl raised her hand. The woman (who looked surprisingly like Tuk) nodded, and the child almost ran to where Lauren stood. In her small, square-fingered hand was a stick-figure picture that was taller than the other figures on the page. "Tee--chur," she said triumphantly.

Lauren knew then that "Teacher" was third-person-singular-feminine to the children of the mission. Men, Father Troy explained later, were "Master." Ideas she must remember for the newsletter!

While Troy spoke briefly with his aide, Mrs. Tulook, Lauren walked between the two rows of children, quietly observing their activities. At first she read suspicion in their liquid eyes. Then, slowly, her presence became funny to them, and here and there a giggle erupted in spite of Mrs. Tulook's warning finger to her lips. *Children are children no matter where they are,* she thought to herself, and gave them an understanding smile.

Kneeling on one knee to examine a piece of artwork, Lauren's eyes locked with eyes darker than her own. The Eskimo boy was drawing a picture almost identical to the one the little girl had shown. "Is this a picture of a teacher?" she asked, pointing to Mrs. Tulook.

The child nodded his head of heavy, straight hair.

"Tee--chur!" He paused and pointed at her, then added shyly, "Like!"

"And I like you too!" she said warmly, and would have put her arm around his shoulders except that she wasn't sure what the customs were here. The child might be embarrassed. Or the others might laugh.

The children got carried away in their good-byes. Lauren tried waving to them as a group. When they continued to chorus "Tee--chur!" she reached out an experimental hand to the small boy nearest to her. When he shook it solemnly, she shook hands with each of the boys. Then, seeing the look of sadness on the faces of the little girls at being ignored, she impulsively went back and hurriedly hugged each one. To her surprise, there was not a giggle in the room.

Once outside, Lauren said, "Was it all right—my reacting as I did? I mean, will the children be scolded for their noisiness?"

"You were wonderful! And, no, the boys and girls will not be scolded. Quite the contrary—they are encouraged to be open always. Different from your American customs, I believe?"

"Yes," she said slowly as they walked the short distance to one of the small houses. "Yes and no. We do express ourselves—sometimes a little *too* openly for my taste. Yet we still hold back. We sublimate."

Troy reached to pull the leather thong at the door and then paused. "In all except matters of the heart you speak freely?"

"Do we appear to draw the line there?"

He nodded. "There seems to be—you will forgive me?—a false openness. Americans seem more willing to discuss lovemaking than love itself."

Lauren felt her face grow warm and wished he would pull the thong. When he did not, she shifted the subject: "I'm glad to see the children so responsive."

"Ah, yes, as your song says, 'What the World Needs Now Is Love, Sweet Love!' "

To Lauren's relief, the door swung open. An elderly lady greeted "Father Troy-ee" with a wide, toothless smile. The smile disappeared when she saw Lauren.

"Miss Eldridge, who has come to help us, Mrs. Chusuk. We have been to the mission," Troy said hastily.

"And I loved your children!" Lauren added.

She knew then that she had earned the right to enter the door of the humble house and had won the woman's heart as well. The visits grew easier as they went to greet one family after another in their pitifully furnished quarters into which sometimes as many as 12 members were crowded. She hoped she could help, as Troy had promised.

★ ★ ★

"Tell me about your book, Lauren. Your aunt says you are a writer," Troy said as they started home.

"Hardly a writer," Lauren smiled. "One of my sociology profs was interested in a paper I wrote on marriage and has promised to help me find a publisher if I'll pursue it."

"And what is it exactly that you are trying to find out?"

"How women across the world make marriage work. It's an evolutionary process, I know, but each must have ways of working at it—"

Lauren paused, feeling somehow that her words were not pleasing to Troy. The narrow road demanded his attention and she was able to study his dark profile. Frowning in concentration, he appeared about to say something. "What are you thinking?" she burst out almost angrily, and then wondered why.

Troy's voice was even when he responded, "That you speak of marriage as if it were a leaky faucet! Something that is constantly in need of repair. That brings a grim picture to mind—a man and a woman, gritting their teeth and twisting defective parts instead of letting love be the natural thing that it is."

"I do not believe that love *is* the natural thing. It is—it has to be—a learned emotion."

"Perhaps," he said softly, and she could feel him shaking his head with regret. "Perhaps what you say is so. But to *work* at marriage? Your American work ethic should leave marriage alone. But then," he inhaled deeply, "it is women you are interviewing! Perhaps I too shall learn from your research."

In the short distance that remained, the two of them were silent, giving Lauren time to contemplate. Bittersweet events of the day came back, and the people and their acceptance of her, soon to be crowded out by Troy's thoughts on marriage and his definition of love. Was there, after all, a microbe of truth in this man's philosophy? Was "doing what comes naturally" what made love glow and marriage grow? It couldn't be that simple. It just couldn't! She and Eric had been "naturals," reading each other's thoughts, never concerning themselves with the unknown factors of a relationship. They just *knew*. And knowing erased that elusive ingredient she was looking for now.

"Do you read Shakespeare?" Lauren looked at Troy as the jeep came to a halt in front of the inn.

"Some," he said. "Why do you ask?"

"I was trying to recall the phrase about not 'bending with the remover to remove.' We just have to bend, period."

He picked up the threads of the conversation effortlessly as if he too had been thinking about it. "That's not what I meant," he said slowly. "Would not that connote the surrender of individual differences, forcing one or the other into passivity? The path of least resistance is not what I had in mind."

"Nor I," Lauren admitted. "It all used to be simple, didn't it? You know, with marriages arranged by families. Or, going back to the parents of us all, Adam and Eve had no problem! *They* never had to figure who would be the ideal mate, Eric said—"

"Eric?"

"Eric is—" she hesitated. What was Eric, anyway? *Brother?* Not that others knew. *Playmate?* No. *Eric was my other self...bone of my bone...flesh of my flesh...Oh no! That was Adam and Eve...*

Lauren realized that Troy was waiting for her to continue. She realized, too, that color had stained her face.

"Eric is my friend!" The words were defensive, a fact that Lauren regretted.

But Troy seemed more concerned with the words than with her tone of voice. "I am glad, my dear." Gently he touched her hand and then stepped from the jeep and came gallantly to help her from the vehicle.

Lauren knew then that she had given another false

impression to this gentle, well-meaning man of God—
not in anything she had said, but in something she had
left *un*said. She knew too that their walking the gra-
veled path shoulder-to-shoulder toward the door of the
inn gave another wrong impression. And, yes, there
was an audience. A drape moved on the front window,
and Lauren was certain that it was Jessica's face she
saw in that split second. Maybe she should have a talk
with Jessica and explain to her what she should have
explained to Troy—that she was about to become
engaged. No, her aunt had extracted a promise:
Lauren was to make no mention of her plans, but just
to relax, see a whole new world, work on her book,
and make the right decisions without advice, interrup-
tions, or interference. And promises were not given
lightly. They were solemn. Even sacred.

"Hurry up, you two! It's mail time."

Lauren had given no thought as yet to mail. The letter she had promised Mother had gone unwritten
because of the flurry of activities here. Mother had
Nella's address, of course, but Ty did not. Lauren had
turned a deaf ear to his every means of cajolery. "I'll
write," she had promised. "But first I need a little
space."

"Well, dear heart, you will get it in Alaska—space
and more! But think fast, won't you? Here are my
cards—addresses and phone numbers where I can be
reached—or will you have a telephone?"

Lauren had not known and still didn't, she realized.
She could only guess that the shortwave radio that
everybody (except herself) knew how to use took the
place of a telephone.

Apparently mail call was one of the day's big events.

All the guests had assembled in the living room when Lauren and Troy walked inside. "One of us makes a trip to the airport even if we're pretty sure the mail plane can't get through—in winter, that is," Nella explained to Lauren, opening the sack in preparation for dumping the contents on a long library table near the entrance.

Lauren wondered later if the events that took place during this time just before dinner were as strange as they appeared, or if they only appeared so to her. First she noticed the silence as Nella made an attempt to sort the stack of mail. There was more than expectancy in the group. There was strain.

"You needn't put the pieces in alphabetical order!" Jessica's voice was sharp, a fact which Nella pointedly ignored.

"Friar!" she called and handed Troy a packet of what appeared to be magazines and possibly school supplies.

Nella picked up two business envelopes, but—to Lauren's complete surprise—before her aunt could announce the name of the addressees, both Jessica and Anna Petrov sprang forward. Jessica made a grab for the airmail envelope, but it was already in Anna's hand. Anna examined it quickly and then handed it back to Nella, who stood well out of Jessica's reach. Jessica, however had examined the other envelope and, with a sly smile, handed it to Anna. As the white envelope changed hands, Lauren had the strange impression that it bore her own handwriting. What a ridiculous thought! Dr. Piriot had warned that Alaska was tricky! She was still shaking her head to make things focus realistically when Nella called her name.

To Lauren's surprise, there was a letter to her from her mother. She almost cried out in joy. Until then she had not realized how much she missed her mother—and home. Turning to see if the others opened their mail here or went their private ways, Lauren failed to hear her aunt call her name again. Vaguely, she was aware that Anna was signing for the white envelope.

Nella laid an envelope in her lap. "Yours, baby," she smiled. It was the airmail envelope Jessica and Anna had tried to intercept! Quickly, unaware at first that she was being observed, Lauren scanned the envelope for a return address. Paris! Ty...*Ty had written*...but how did he know where to find her?

It would be good to hear from Ty, to be reassured that she was wanted and desired. She laid the letter on top of her mother's, making sure that the ends were perfectly aligned. When she lifted her eyes, Lauren became aware that two pairs of eyes were focused upon her—Anna's, in well-bred amusement at her concentration with the arrangement of the letters in her lap (or did the faint lift of the silvery brows ask a question?), and Jessica's! Jessica's expression was easy to interpret. The thick-lashed lids were lowered so that her ice-blue eyes scarcely showed in the caramel features of her beautiful face. How could a girl with so much hatred in her heart hope to make a success of a marriage with a priest? Good question!

Lauren realized then that the others were leaving. "I—I guess I'm a little pooped from today," she admitted to Nella. "I need a long, soaking bath. Would you mind terribly if I skipped dinner?"

"You are. You do. And I would!" her aunt said.

Chapter Five

Ty's letter was all that she should expect, but Lauren found it incomplete and puzzling. She scanned it quickly, looking for something that was not there. What was she hoping to find, anyway? She didn't know for sure, but she would recognize it. Biting the knuckle of her left forefinger in concentration, slowly she began to reread the letter.

My Darling:

By now surely you have come to your senses and are ready to leave your self-imposed exile in that northern wilderness. You spoke once of not wishing to "abandon" your mother. Have you not abandoned her already? There are a number of arrangements which would provide for her care and free you from the responsibility— once we are married. I am not a patient

man. I must therefore caution you that I
shall find you wherever you go and, finding you, I shall follow! As the "green-
apple" song goes, "If that's not love..."
And so, come home—or I shall come there.

> Adoringly,
>
> Ty

P.S. You *did* mail my letter in Seattle?
Good girl!

The letter needed more thought than she had,
Lauren realized as she consulted her watch. Nella, like
Mother, was a split-second timer when it came to
meals. There was little more than time to read
Mother's letter as it was. But what was it that Ty had
said? That she had *abandoned* her mother? He didn't
understand, and the accusation was unfair. Abandon-
ing was more what Ty *himself* was suggesting.
"Arrangements" indeed! As if her mother were a piece
of outdated furniture to be disposed of! Nobody could
understand, of course, how she felt about her mother
and Eric felt about his father. Except for the two
children, maybe their parents could have reached the
kind of solution that did not lead to the breaking of
one of God's commandments. Well, the responsibility
for her mother's emotional well-being was there
whether Ty liked it or not. He would have to get used
to it.

Resolutely Lauren picked up Roberta Eldridge's
letter. Then she laid it back down. Her momentary
pique at Ty's reference to a member of her family
whom he had not even met gave way to curiosity and
then to a strange foreboding. How had Ty found her

whereabouts? And his avowal to find and follow her sounded more like a threat than a promise. Then the letter! Probably she would have put it out of her mind had Ty not referred to it again. But obviously it was important.

"What do you know of this man? Really *know?*" her aunt had written, a question which she pointedly had ignored. "Well, maybe I'd better face it now." Lauren said the words aloud in the empty room and half-expected to hear an answer. The room suddenly didn't seem empty anymore, a feeling which left her uncomfortable. The climate *was* tricky. What else could account for such unworthy thinking? Determinedly, Lauren ripped open the other envelope.

Lauren scanned the contents quickly as she had with Ty's, smiling as she read her mother's light-touched way of dealing with not-so-pleasant material. The world would have proven unbearable to her laid out in its black-and-white truth, Lauren thought a little sadly.

Mother had been sick, Lauren was sure. Her friends had contracted "something they described as 'ghastly-awful,' a virus," but Mother had a "slight cold—nothing to sniffle about." The movers had trouble with loading the refrigerator—"The door kept opening invitingly." The men kept kicking it shut, but Uncle Fred advised them to reason with the machine.

Misty-eyed, Lauren was about to lay her mother's letter aside when she came to the final paragraph. There, as she read, her heart skipped a beat, seemed to stop altogether, and then began to beat furiously against her ribs.

> The questionnaires are coming back for
> you, darling, and I will send them by
> separate cover. But I thought you only
> mailed them out to women. Imagine my
> surprise at Eric's responding! I opened it
> through mistake, as it was the only one ad-
> dressed to me. I am glad I did, as he asked
> for your address. That surprised me, since
> the two of you are so close. How did you
> ever forget—or did he lose it? Now you
> take care, kitten....

Eric! Eric wanted her address. Lauren felt the first
real surge of joy she had sensed for a long time. Why,
she and Eric *never* wrote. They simply waited for the
summers...but he was going to write now, and it
couldn't be to send the questionnaire...Lauren
laughed at his having completed the form. She had
only shown it to him for his approval as he had shared
the outline for his dissertation with her. But now Eric
was going to write!

Nella called Lauren very early on Sunday morning.
Tuk's fluffy, golden-brown, sourdough pancakes
served with wild raspberry syrup was well worth getting up for. "But why the early rising?" she wondered
aloud.

"For church services. We all attend," Nella explained, passing the syrup pitcher to Lauren again.

"This is wonderful," Lauren said with appreciation,
and helped herself generously to the contents of the
glass pitcher.

"You're going to enjoy the service to the utmost,
I see," Dr. Piriot said with amusement in his voice.

"The syrup's laced with hooch, you know."

"Hooch? You mean," she said slowly, "it has liquor in it?"

"Are you afraid of corrupting your morals, Miss Eldridge—Lauren?" Jessica spoke the words lightly, but the sarcasm was thinly veiled. "Or spoiling that paper-doll figure?"

Lauren bit down hard on her pancake to hold back a rush of angry words. The other girl's rudeness was uncalled-for. Driving the harpoon in was never enough; Jessica had to give it a twist.

Troy saved the moment by explaining, "The American slang expression comes from *hootchenoo*—Indian origin, I believe?" He looked around the table, but nobody seemed to know. "Anyhow, it originated here some two centuries ago. Mixture of molasses, dried fruits, and local berries. Distilled, it makes a palatable but potent drink. Popular with the parishioners, but not exactly suitable for communion!"

Lauren finished her coffee and excused herself, saying lightly that she needed to sober up before the ride up the mountain.

"*Down* the mountain," her aunt corrected. "Sundays are busy for Father Troy. He conducts services at the airport in the morning. Then in the afternoons he ministers to the people *up* the mountain."

"We all do," Troy said quietly.

Lauren caught Anna's eye and smiled. To her surprise, the girl spoke in her deep-throated way, "True. Miss Trusdale and the others are sort of missionaries here."

"Hardly that," Nella objected. "We take clothes—ours and those which arrive through World Missions.

It's more of an exchange program than a missionary project, I'm afraid. The people insist on supplying our fish and game. Then there are the furs and skins— plenty for our parkas, a winter necessity here.''

"But you aren't prepared to stay the winter, are you, Miss Eld—uh, Lauren?" *She's stumbling over my name purposely,* Lauren thought. *I've prayed—and I'll keep on praying—that I can overlook your behavior, Jessica.*

Aloud, she said, "If by 'prepared' you mean *planning* to spend the winter, yes, I am. But as to being prepared clothing-wise, no." Then, on sudden inspiration, she added, "I was hoping you could help me."

Jessica's face reddened at the turn-of-cheek words. "Now I really must be getting ready—*after* I sober up." Lauren smiled at the group, fluttered a fingertip farewell, and hurried down the hall.

Nella had the motor of the jeep running when Lauren, in a lightweight blue suit, came out. Her aunt pointed with a grin and wink at Jessica, who was seated—*snuggled* would have been more like it—beside Troy in the other jeep, her cloud of dark hair, gently responding to the morning breeze, blowing across his face. Mismatched though they appeared to be in the important things, they made a handsome pair.

There were more houses near the airport than Lauren had realized when she came in a week before. Most of the men, she learned, helped out in one way or another with maintenance, keeping the runway in good repair, and taking care of the few other planes which brought in supplies and mail. Fortunately, Nella explained, one of the wives was a teacher and tutored the few children. Father Troy had started a little

Bible study, and families got together once a week for discussion. Then he came himself on Sunday mornings. Services were in the hangar.

"They're all from the continental U.S.," she finished as they neared the door of the hangar. "Kakalota residents are Eskimo and Indian. Different beliefs, practices, cultures. Only 40 miles separates them, but they're worlds apart. Of course," lowering her voice, "sometimes we're that far apart even when we're side-by-side, you know? It's like we move to new surroundings but leave our hearts behind."

Lauren glanced quickly at her aunt but saw no indication that her words were anything more than a chance remark.

Lauren tried to concentrate on the service but found her mind wandering back to Nella's words. *I'm like that,* she thought. *My heart has never changed environments once. Not even once! It's been on the beach, building sand castles, then crawling into one of them to live and die, since that day...*

Digging her nails into her palms, she forced herself to sit up straighter and listen to what Troy was reading. His words came, she discovered, from a little black book the others held. It was a prayer book of some kind, but there seemed to be no other copies.

"I gathered you didn't get much from the service?" Nella asked as they drove back to the inn.

"It was different," Lauren said slowly. "I guess I need a sermon—not so much reading."

"Understandable with your background!"

"I didn't know I *had* a background," Lauren said in surprise.

"For all the talking your family has always done,

it seems to me that there's been a lot left unsaid," Nella observed.

"For sure," Lauren agreed. "And this background of mine?"

"Baptist. Good old shouting Baptist. 'Primitive,' I believe they called themselves. Straight from the Blue Ridge Mountains—on our side of the family, that is. Why, Grandpa was Deacon Trusdale, member of the group who called themselves 'Hardshell.' He's *the* Deacon Trusdale who drove the missionaries out. Threatened to tar and feather them—but surely you've heard this?"

Lauren leaned forward eagerly. "I have not. Please go on."

Nella laughed. "I can't tell whether you're shocked or amused."

"Mostly surprised at this point."

"And *that* is the surprising part—seeing that you're a throwback."

The idea jarred Lauren somehow. "Now, you know I wouldn't—"

"Of course you wouldn't. And you haven't heard half of it. Still, there *is* a certain quality—"

"Of piety? Self-righteousness? Oh, I hope not! That would be terribly misleading—"

"I meant what I said as a compliment. Just stay as you are. What you have makes you winsome and totally charming."

"Thank you, Nella. I guess I needed to hear something like that. But," she hesitated, not wishing to hurt her aunt's feelings, "it's just that being winsome and charming, as you phrase it, has nothing to do with *faith*."

Her aunt changed gear for the hill ahead. "Well, now, I could debate that point. We 'Primitives' believe in shouting out the Word, and I can assure you that how the messenger looks and acts is mighty important in getting others to hear the words above the noise!"

Lauren relaxed a bit. "You just may have a point—"

"But you want to hear more about Grandpa?"

Lauren laughed. "Exactly."

"The old gent opposed the missionaries because they were too educated. Said they were so busy trying to decide which Bible passages were fact and which were figures of speech that they never did get the point of *any* of it. 'If it's in the Good Book, it's so, and you so-and-so's ain't tellin' me otherwise even if you're *educated* so-and-so's—so git!' and the story goes that they got!"

It was good to talk like this. Now Lauren realized how much she had missed as she grew up, and she wished for the thousandth time that her parents had been a little more conservative in their views of life, love, and marriage—*particularly* marriage. But immediately she felt disloyal. She had loved her parents dearly...but what had gone wrong?

"Nella," she said slowly, "what happened to Mother and Daddy? They stopped going to church altogether. Do you know when? Or why?"

"No, I don't, baby. Fact is, it's news to me that they *did* stop. They—your mother, rather—loved church and took a big part. Of course, the marriage was a mistake from the beginning."

Lauren felt her head jerk erect. She didn't want to miss a word. Nella just might hold the key to mysteries surrounding her past. Then, to her disappointment, she realized that they were back at the inn. "We must talk again, Nella—please."

"Indeed, we must! And I want to hear all about this Ty—what's his name?"

"Ty. Tyrone Valdez." Lauren marveled at how the very mention of his name could send the blood rushing to her fingertips. She loked down at her hands, half-expecting to see little blue blazes at the tip of each rosy, oval-shaped nail. No blazes. But her hands trembled.

Tuk's square face, lighted by the usual broad smile, appeared at the door. "Meal read--eee, Boss Lad--eee!"

"And so are we, eh, gang?" Nella called.

The group scrambled forward, sat down, and waited for Father Troy's prayer. Lauren had hoped to work on her book during the afternoon, but the others seemed to take it for granted that she would go along with them to the Kakalota services.

Lauren saw some of the same faces she had seen earlier in the week, and she met several other people. Dr. Piriot introduced three men whom he identified as trappers. The men were dressed in outdoor clothing, including heavy boots, and appeared ill-at-ease. To her surprise, they seemed to make a point of speaking first to Jessica and then to Anna and Ivan, carrying on a low-toned conversation. Without any real interest, Lauren wondered just what any of them could have in common. She then forgot the incident, because after Troy's reading what seemed to be the same book he had used at the morning service (except that it was in French), he dismissed with a short benediction and the children surrounded her. *Tee--chur, tee--chur!"*

The next week seemed to fly past. Troy, Dr. Piriot, and Lauren spent a morning planning the kinds of things to include in the newsletter—or letters, because as they talked the three of them decided it would be good to publish two. One would be a rebus-type information sheet for the Kakalota residents. On these, Lauren would express words and phrases by pictures of objects whose names resembled the words in the messages the two men wished to convey. She would fill in the other words with the ancient manual typewriter which was at her disposal, using both French and English languages.

The other newsletter would go to the English-speaking people at the airport. There would be no problem in communicating with them. "But just maybe we can bring the three worlds together this way—theirs, ours, and that of Kakalota." Dr. Piriot added that they would need the same medical advice he hoped to get across to the mountainfolk. And Lauren had some thoughts of her own. *Wouldn't it be nice if the radio set brought in world news and weather reports, and wouldn't it be exciting if there were some way to arrange for personal messages to be sent out and received?* She knew nothing of radio communicating, but surely they did. The ideas they shared were challenging and exciting.

"Of course, at this point I can offer little more than enthusiasm," Lauren apologized.

"Inspiration is more nearly the word," Troy assured her appreciatively.

Lauren was grateful for the long daylight hours and extended her workday to a minimum of 12 hours, a fact that she carefully concealed. Nella, Dr. Piriot, and

Troy would join forces against her program, not understanding the driving urge within her to do an excellent job. Sometimes she was unable to understand it herself.

"Each reader's going to need the Rosetta stone to figure out my hieroglyphics, demotic characters, French, and English. Have a look at this mumbo jumbo!" Lauren had laughed, hoping that her offhand manner gave no indication of how many hours she had spent trying to get a few medical suggestions and a Bible verse into something the readers could understand.

The first newsletter was a far cry from what any of them hoped to publish later. Lauren was aware that a long struggle lay ahead. But she had no doubt that she was up to the challenge. Practice, along with trial and error, would smooth out the imperfections in time.

But some inner force compelled her to push almost beyond endurance—a force having nothing to do with the rough spots in the mechanics of the newsletter. A perfectionist by nature, Lauren was accustomed to putting in overtime on any undertaking. But what plagued her now was a vague fear that time was running out. How ridiculous! But no amount of reasoning with herself erased the sense of urgency. There was something to accomplish and not enough time to finish it— not unless she hurried. And so she drove herself, working compulsively.

Was it possible that newcomers tried to store Alaska's summer light away for the winter darkness? Impossible as it sounded, soon now—mid-August, didn't Nella say?—Arctic winds would blow back the Pacific's warmer air mass. Summer, with its 20 hours of daylight, would surrender to winter with its five or six. "And even the daylight's not what you'd expect," Nella had warned. "There's no visible sun—just a hint of a glint, like the sun's hibernating behind Mount McKinley! It's other-worldly. A planet of blue-shadowed mystery. Vast. Silent. Endless hills of mounded snow stretching out into eternity."

Her aunt's description of the landscape had sent little chills of elation up and down Lauren's spine. See-ing an Alaskan winter promised to be an experience of a lifetime, no matter what dangers came with it, but the feeling of urgency had roots in something deeper—some emotion closer to her heart. And it bothered Lauren that she was unable to identify it.

"Say, now, you are doing a superb job!" Dr. Piriot picked up one of the communique's and inspected it with satisfaction. In the three weeks that they had worked on the project, Lauren had enlarged it from business-size stationery to legal-form length, and to-day for the first time she had utilized both the front and back sides of the paper.

"Does my illustration put across the idea of poisonous medicines?"

"It's excellent," he said, examining the skull-and-crossbones symbol. "And Father Troy's words about 'Throwing Away the Old' parallels it perfectly. Tell me, Lauren, can you draw a picture of a mink?"

Lauren considered and then said, "I don't think I know for sure what they look like, except for the fur."

"They're weasel-like, web-footed. I had a fatality yesterday from a bite that one of the villagers sus-tained when he tried to capture one of the animals. They're dangerous, and the people need to know it."

"I'm sorry—was it a trapper who was bitten?"

"No, although I suppose the family would have saved the fur. It was the meat they wanted, however."

Lauren gulped. "Should they eat such foods?"

The doctor's eyes twinkled. "The clean and the unclean are Father Troy's department. I'll stick to binding up wounds."

Lauren had come to admire Troy Huguenot tremendously during the past two months. No wonder the villagers loved and respected him! His acceptance of the people as they were, instead of trying to change their culture, and his determined devotion were sermon enough. Feeling as they did about their leader, the men, women, and children would strive to comprehend the newsletters. Their hearts were warmed, she was sure, by the knowledge that somebody as "important" as their beloved Father Troy cared enough to bother with its publication on their behalf. That knowledge thrilled her more than she would have thought possible. Her stay here had turned out quite differently than expected. "I came for adventure, in spite of the fact that you thought I needed rest," Lauren had teased her aunt. "But I got more than I bargained for—involvement. I wouldn't have suspected that I could care so much."

"You also came for escape," Nella said. "Always a little tricky. Look at what happened to Jonah."

There was nothing to escape, Lauren had wanted to object. But Troy had walked in and asked for her help just as she was about to speak. "I'm having difficulty," he said, puckering his brow faintly. "I want to use Jesus' parable of the 99 sheep—"

"How can I help?"

"Alas!" Troy said helplessly. "These people never saw a sheep."

Lauren laughed. "Use a reindeer!"

But Troy did not laugh. "Of course," he said. "But of course! If you will sketch one for us—"

Lauren groaned. "And *I* have never seen a reindeer!"

The idea came to her then—or at least it surfaced. Lauren suspected that the thought had lurked in her mind for a long time, just biding time until its release. "What would you think of our letting the children at the mission help on this? As a matter of fact, I'm still trying to come up with a picture of a mink for Dr. Piriot."

"What would I think? I would applaud the idea, my dear, long and very loudly. We might even let the children initial the drawings. They could use the recognition."

Lauren warmed to the idea. "And if we took some copies of this newsletter to the children at the airport?" she said experimentally.

Troy's eyes lit up. "Maybe the children down below would write notes of appreciation."

"We can suggest pen pals!" A glow of excitement that began somewhere in the region of her heart spread over Lauren's entire body. She felt exhilarated and inspired. God was speaking to her as He had never spoken to her before. For the first time, she was experiencing the thrill that can come only through unselfish service.

So involved was she with the escalating project that when the days began to shorten she scarcely noticed. Still urged on by the force within, Lauren simply switched on the lights and continued to work on the summer schedule. The questionnaires that Mother had promised had not come. Eager as she was to get back to the book, Lauren was pleased at the delay. Right now the newsletter took all her time—either doing the actual paper or making related trips to Kakalota or the airport. She and the two men used the travel time for planning, which made scheduling easier for them all.

"You have made a remarkable adjustment here, my dear Lauren," Troy said in his usual polite, carefully-precise voice after one of the many trips up the mountain road. "It was indeed intended that you should come here, that we should meet, and that you should stay."

"That I should come here, yes, I believe that. As to my staying—that remains to be seen."

"Ah," his voice was gentle, "and you avoided the most important of the three. I spoke of us."

"Troy," Lauren bit her lip in concentration. "There's something I should have told you a long time ago—"

Troy looked into her eyes and spoke sadly, "Must you? Your secret has waited this long. Let us continue as we are for now. I shall not make a nuisance of myself. You have my promise."

The humble words tore at her heart. "Oh, Troy!" she cried out and realized that tears were streaming down her cheeks. "You are so good—so much more than I deserve—"

Gently, Troy put his arms around her, smoothing a stray copper curl from her forehead and talking as one talks to a distraught child. "That is very kind of you, dear, dear Lauren. It is more than I deserve."

He inhaled deeply and then said in a desperate whisper, "Even were this so, we do not love others for their goodness, but for themselves."

"But I admire you—respect you—and I do love you in a special way."

"Oh, Lauren, little Lauren," he said with pain in his voice. "Stop *working* at it. You cannot, in spite of what you would like to believe, select the right person and *learn* to love! Both of us know that my loving you would never be enough."

Neither of them spoke for a moment. It was Lauren who broke the silence. "I must have time to think—that's why I came to Alaska. It's not as simple as you think."

She should have told him then about Ty...her doubts...Eric...their relationship...her parents, and her consequent doubts about marrying *anybody*. It would have eased his pain and perhaps purged her of the burden she carried in her own heart. But just as she would have poured out the words, there was a faint shuffle of footsteps at the door of the living room where the two of them were standing. Lauren glanced up quickly from the shelter of Troy's arms to see Jessica's flashing eyes on them. Then the girl turned and was gone.

Later in the week, Lauren made a point of watching for Jessica entering her room alone. Following her a few minutes later, Lauren tapped lightly on the door.

When Jessica opened it, her dark hair showing burnished strands beneath the glow of the ceiling light, Lauren thought again how lovely the girl was. Lovely and brilliant, but watchful, suspicious, and unhappy.

"Yes?" Jessica's voice made no attempt at friendliness.

"We've never had a real opportunity to get ac-
quainted," Lauren began. "May I come in?"

"Why?" Jessica asked bluntly.

"Why, to talk—"

Jessica had little recourse but to wave an arm of invitation but there was no warmth in the gesture.
Clearly there was nothing to talk about.

Just inside the door Lauren hesitated. "Maybe I
shouldn't have come," she said uncertainly.

"If you've come about Troy, forget it. I intend to
win, you know."

"It's no contest, Jessica," Lauren said, fighting for
her self-control. "I have other plans for my private
life."

"That tender scene I witnessed meant nothing at all?
Oh, come now, Lauren, you don't expect me to believe
that?"

"I hope you will. We would all be happier that
way."

Jessica moved toward the door purposefully. The
visit was over. "I will be happy either way—providing
you understand it's strictly hands-off. Is that understood?"

Lauren felt a prickle of anger along the back of her
neck. "You need not try to make *me* understand. Concentrate on Troy!"

Immediately she regretted having spoken. Oh, Jessica had it coming. But Lauren saw that by voicing
her own feelings, she had furnished fuel for the flame
of the other girl's jealous fury. She knew then that
Jessica would find a means of getting even. Turning,

Lauren would have murmured an apology, but the door slammed shut in her face.

In the weeks that followed, Lauren tried to steer clear of Jessica. Obviously they could never be friends, but why should they become enemies? She would give the girl no cause, since even her presence seemed to be an irritation. To Jessica she was the intruder, the only obstacle between her and Troy.

That being the case, it would be best to avoid being alone with him as much as possible. When she repeatedly gave excuses at his invitations, Troy looked concerned and then hurt.

"I do hope that I have in no way offended you, Lauren."

"Oh no, of course not!"

"Then you must come with me. The children are asking, as are their parents. It is a fine thing you are doing, and I believe you will agree we must put their needs ahead of all else?"

Troy was right. It was with misgiving, however, that she resumed their former schedule. Jessica was sure to read something into it and, unless Lauren missed her guess, the girl was of a vindictive nature. And to further complicate matters, Troy was becoming more attentive in spite of her efforts to discourage him. Confusing. Even frightening.

If only Eric would write, she thought, *it would put me back in touch with the real world out there.* She had watched the mail every day, hoping against hope, that his promised letter would come. Several times she thought of asking Mother what caused the delay, but something held her back. Guilt maybe. After all, shouldn't she be looking for another letter from Ty instead of a message from Eric? There had been no further word since his one letter, and she had been unable to respond because there was no return address.

The air turned sharp and cold. "There can be a blizzard any day now," Nella warned. "I've been thinking about warm clothes for you."

"I guess I didn't expect the season to be so short," Lauren admitted. "Where and when can we shop? Are things as high-priced as I hear?"

"There's no place close by for shopping, but we could manage to go into the city. As to the cost, out of sight—but *not* out of mind! It's awfully impractical to outfit yourself unless you're convinced you'll be staying."

"Not forever!" Lauren was surprised to hear herself respond so quickly and with so much feeling. What *did* she plan to do? It would depend on Ty and his plans, wouldn't it? She wasn't sure of anything.

"Well, then, why not come into my private shop and take your pick? I have more heavy boots, socks, and parkas than we two can ever wear out."

When Nella opened her closet door, Lauren could not resist a laugh. "You mean you actually wear *these?* Your tailor must have known about Tuk's cooking and left you room to grow!"

Nella smiled and then sobered. "We have little regard for style here, except for dinner. The object is survival, and to survive at 40 to 80 degrees below zero takes layers of clothing if not the fat."

Lauren felt her blood curdle. "Did you mean that about the temperature?"

"We're in the Arctic, baby. The land's impersonal. Here before we came. Here after we go. It's uncon-

querable, but not uninhabitable. Let's put it this way:
How much time elapses between our entrance and our
exit very well may depend on how strictly we adhere
to its rules. Doc will lay down quite a few, I suspect.
But clothing's my department. Now, let's give you the
layered look. Still in, isn't it?''

Lauren nodded numbly, then outfitted herself in
layer after layer of her aunt's heavy garments, ending
up with boots surely manufactured for a walk in space.
She was aghast when she saw herself in the mirror.

"I can't breathe, let alone walk!"

"You'll not be walking much. We'll be switching
to snowmobiles. Above Kakalota they'll make use of
the dogsleds.''

It was hard to believe. But even as Lauren peeled
off the scratchy clothing she realized that her aunt had
switched on the ceiling light. Back in her own quarters,
she opened the drapes and looked out on a world she
hardly recognized. The long, gray fingers of twilight
reached out to tangle shadows where there appeared
to be nowhere to cast them. The scene was unreal and
frightening, not at all akin to the intimacy of the wispy
fogs of the California shores. The cold would come.
Already she felt it like a rim of frost around her heart.

Chapter Six

There were no warning flakes to say that winter was approaching—just a sudden, impenetrable wall of snow. Visibility zero. In the shadowy, blue-gray half-light the wall revealed strange humps like miniature igloos heaped with snow. Other shapes, outside the small section of Lauren's window which was not iced over, were unrecognizable. Pale violet lights seemed to poke at the wide spaces between the distant snow-burdened hills. Truly magnificent! one part of her whispered. A second part lured her with a certain sense of adventure. But the third part warned of danger. Try as she would to put the feeling aside, it persisted and became a foreboding, having to do with something more than the weather.

The newsletter had kept Lauren so busy that she was scarcely aware of the other comings and goings around the inn. She was surprised to have Dr. Piriot offer to show her how to use the shortwave system which he and Troy had put into operation for emergency use.

"Are you familiar with the use of the radio?"

When Lauren told him she was not, he said, "It's simple. You will need to receive and send out messages. All of us help on a 24-hour shift."

"I'm glad," she told him. "I had hoped we could have some means of communicating for our little newspaper."

"And I too. But we must be prepared in case of illness, accident, quakes, or a glacier storm."

"Will we be able to assist or to leave at all times?"

"We hope so," he said quietly. "There will be many a need."

The words should have been reassuring, but Lauren felt a certain claustrophobia. A momentary vision of California's wide-open spaces passed before her eyes.

"You'll need some orientation before your first trip in one of the snowmobiles." Grateful to have her mind occupied, Lauren listened to the doctor's warnings about proper clothing, breathing, exercise, and diet. She made copious notes and promised to study them.

The initial storm passed. The snow must have melted somewhat, because long, silvery icicles hung—like translucent bars from the windows. "I am a prisoner here," Lauren found herself saying aloud in her room, "a prisoner in a castle of ice."

Such thinking could make a person a good candidate for wild imaginings. And surely she had to be imagining some of the strange events that took shape around her.

She was not imagining the ice *inside* the inn! The morning Lauren discovered it on the panes of the hall windows, she was amazed. "Is it really ice? What can we do?" she asked Nella.

"It's really ice and there's little we can do but wait for the spring thaw," her aunt said comfortably. "We have to conserve the heat, so the halls are the coldest. You'll get used to it."

Lauren looked at the Dr. Zhivago world around her and wondered if she ever would get used to it. But what was happening on the inside concerned her even more. During several nights she thought she had heard footsteps outside her door, as she had when she first came to the inn. But there was never any evidence of another person's presence. "Probably the wind," Nella said, showing no concern.

When the sound came again, Lauren summoned her courage and flung the door wide open without taking time for her robe. Only the cold silence of the hall greeted her—wait! There was something more. Not a motion, but an odor so pungent in its tart-sweetness that the inn might have been surrounded by orange groves.

"Is fresh fruit hard to come by?" Lauren asked at the table one evening.

"Almost impossible," Troy told her. "We have ordered a good supply of dried fruits, however." The answer told her nothing.

Again and again the haunting odor came—always from the hall, it seemed, except for the one time that one of the spare blankets on her bed during a blizzard had the same aroma. The odor was so heady that Lauren drifted off to sleep on the magic carpet of her childhood, causing her to dream of oranges springing out of the snow and Eskimo children gathering them in. A dream, of course. It was all a dream.

And then came her mysterious finding which could

neither be shrugged off as imagination nor explained away as a dream. Having trouble one morning with the closing of her parka, Lauren hurried down the hall for Nella to give her a hand. The temperature had dropped still lower during the night, and Dr. Piriot's instructions were to add an extra layer of clothing.

Just before reaching her aunt's door, Lauren stepped on something round and hard, causing her boot to career crazily. As she knelt to feel her ankle and make sure there was no sprain, her eyes caught sight of a small object in the animal-skin rug. It was hard to see in the semidarkness, but she managed in cold-fingered awkwardness to find the object. It was a ring, as best she could tell.

"Was that you stumbling around out here? Get inside before you freeze!"

Lauren obeyed, and for some unexplainable reason she buried the ring in the pocket of her parka.

Nella capably adjusted the fastener. As she worked, Lauren wondered if the faint smell of tobacco was another figment of her imagination. It was becoming hard to separate fantasy from truth.

"Why so pensive?" Nella asked suddenly.

Lauren started guiltily, then made her voice purposely light, "I was wondering how long you'd been smoking a pipe."

It was her aunt's turn to look startled. "Oh, uh," she fumbled for words, "oh, yes, I remember now. Uh—Dr. Piriot—brought these for you."

Crossing the room quickly, Nella picked up an extra pair of gloves. Lauren wondered why he hadn't brought them directly to her room if they were that important. Then she dismissed the matter from her mind and accepted the heavy, loosely woven, woolen gloves.

Turning, Lauren was about to leave when she caught sight of her aunt's face. Off guard, Nella looked a little uncertain and afraid—no, sad—causing Lauren to say, "You know, I never did ask you the same question you asked me. Do *you* intend to stay here in Alaska?"

Nella's face came alive then. "Oh, yes! I'm a part of it. I was never the typical lady—Nimrod who goes actively gunning for a man. On the other hand, I didn't choose to move into a bachelor apartment and furnish it with lavender upholstery and lace curtains!"

"And Alaska was a nice compromise?"

"Perfect! I'm the typical lady with the frozen smile." *(That hides a broken heart,* she might as well have added.)

There was no time to continue the conversation, as Dr. Piriot let Lauren know with a toot of the horn that snowmobile and driver were ready for the icy climb to Kakalota.

The doctor opened the storm door and then the outer door, letting in a blast of Arctic air such as Lauren had never experienced before. It was like a stinging blow against her face, threatening to suck away her very breath. Her nostrils felt paralyzed.

"Cover your mouth with the scarf—*quickly!*" Dr. Piriot ordered.

She obeyed and felt the scarf stiffen with her frozen breath.

"It'll get better. Here, you'd better sit in the middle. We're used to the climate."

Lauren saw then, to her surprise, that Jessica waited

beside the snowmobile. This was no time to struggle with emotions, so she hurried to the waiting vehicle, accepted the blanket Jessica offered, and climbed in, grateful for the warmth of the heater.

"How is your book coming?" Jessica inquired in an effort, Lauren was sure, to effect politeness in the presence of her uncle.

"I'm afraid I've fallen behind hopelessly," Lauren admitted stiffly.

"A fact which we must remedy," the doctor said. "You have been spending too many hours on the publication, but it will be less demanding now. If only Father Troy will not overpersuade you to assist him at the mission. The aides are of no help with English, you know."

"I've only taught Sunday school," Lauren said quickly.

"Exactly the right qualifications, I'm afraid. But this book—tell me now, how can my niece and I be of assistance?"

"Oh, thank you," Lauren said warmly. "That's kind—of you both." She glanced at Jessica and wondered if the other girl's expressive face was a little less hostile. Certainly it was beautiful, with the wind whipping added color to the part of her face that was visible inside the circle of becoming fur. Perhaps Jessica sensed the glance of admiration as she smiled faintly.

Lauren smiled back and then continued, "I'm not sure either of you can help, however. The 50-question survey went out to 1000 persons, but they were women—married women."

The doctor chuckled. "Discriminating, aren't you?

What's wrong with men participating?"

"Because it's about you!" Lauren said quickly and then blushed. "I mean about husbands."

The doctor looked at her sideways. "I was married," he said with a hint of sadness. "My wife succumbed to pneumonia. Your aunt and she were friends."

"I'm sorry—I didn't know—"

"It was a long time ago," he said gently. "And as to my niece—her husband was killed in Vietnam."

"That, too, was a long time ago," Jessica said quickly. "What's the title and main thrust? It *is* a book?"

"A book, yes, eventually, based on women's opinion of all the facets of marriage, but mostly on how it's affected by religion, or rather by religious faith. The title is *Amen to the Altar.*"

"Nice title," the other girl murmured, "but obviously you don't want to hear from those of us who might shatter brides' illusions that they've made a final pact with God...entered into the ultimate bargain, paid the supreme price—doing more than exchanging vows! They've swapped virginity for the blind hope that they'll never be alone again. Then *poof!* It's all over. Men simply aren't an extension of women."

"And therin lies the illusion?" the doctor's tone was slightly mocking, but it carried a note of concern. "Must you be so bitter, Jessica?"

Jessica's answer, if she made one, was lost to Lauren, who was busy trying to sort out her thoughts. Jessica had revealed a side of herself that she had kept under careful wraps. She was opinionated, but she was also hurt and vulnerable. Was that vulnerability what made her so calculating in choosing a second mate? *Actually, we have lot in common,* Lauren thought. *Her own mistakes, like the mistakes of my mother and father, have made us afraid of life.* Maybe she had been as calculating as Jessica...seeking out a man she could love...rejecting the one who loved her...and deep down inside longing for the man who fulfilled both needs. Only it didn't work that way. That was the "illusion." And certainly it made more sense to try to win a man's love than attempt to make herself love against her will.

It was easy to understand why Jessica was bitter. Lauren herself would be too except that God had heard her prayers and softened the bitter core within her. There was no undoing what her father and Eric's mother had done. Their love—no, their passion!—had created the person in whom Lauren found everything—the man who knew all the stars and the constellations and called them all by name. The man who held a piece of her heart in his hand, where it would linger forever, making it impossible to give her whole heart to another man—but who could never claim her as his own because of the Scripture that the two of them had wept over so bitterly as children..."visiting the iniquity of the father unto the third and fourth generation..." *Oh, Eric!*

Lauren was unaware that two great tears formed and would have fallen except that they froze against her lashes. Dr. Piriot spotted them when the vehicle stopped at the edge of the village.

Covering her eyes with a heavy kerchief, he ushered her quickly into the trading post. She had forgotten his caution about snow blindness.

"I should have had you wear snow shields," he scolded himself. "Now, stand still. I must examine you for frostbite." Deftly, with practiced fingers, Dr. Piriot went over all the areas of exposed skin looking for, he explained, the telltale marks of yellowish white.

When at length he said with relief, "You're all right—this time," Jessica motioned from the door to indicate the house they were to visit. "I hope to pick up some terms here for you today, and I needed you with me. If all goes well, Jessica and I can handle it from now on. We've come to depend on your communications so very much."

"Thank you," Lauren answered simply. "Knowing you—getting to understand this part of God's world—has meant more to me than I can say. However," she smiled, "I can't deny that it would be nice to thaw out, relax, and think of this being my last trip up the impossible 'glass hill.' "

"I've a feeling 'twill not be your last," Dr. Piriot spoke with a twinkle in his eyes. "Our Father Troy will go over my head."

"I will come—or go—where I am needed," she agreed as Jessica pulled the thong at the door of the small hut, almost obscured by snow. "Odd, isn't it, how I suddenly feel this terrible sense of urgency to accomplish so much in a limited time and space? A stranger struggling to make it in an alien world?"

"No," he whispered quietly. "Not odd at all. That's the way it is when we hear the Lord call."

Lauren went through the remainer of the day in the kind of white maze of snow and whiteness of mind that she had come to expect. In an almost-detached manner she watched the bright, expectant eyes of the children fix upon her, and she went through the motions of responding warmly—responding with her heart but without feeling in the nerve endings. It must be some kind of adaptation she was making.

"It's remarkable how they react to you," Dr. Piriot said in one of the short trips between the icicled huts. "You have given them strength. 'If Tee--chur say I can do, I can do!' It shows in their eyes."

"Don't make me cry again!" Lauren warned, her head and shoulders hunched against the wind. The vision of the beautiful, dark-eyed children would linger with her for a lifetime no matter where she went. Their sincerity...their unquestioning faith...their total absorption with any task at hand. They sat with brilliant brown eyes aglow in their fur-lined parkas, looking for all the world like tiny velvet mice wanting to love and be loved. But, oh, how easily—how very easily—that trust could turn to fear. It was an awesome responsibility. At the door of every house she whispered, "Make my path straight, Lord—as straight and direct as the paths these people have shoveled between their doors."

The three of them were quiet during the breathtaking descent. Any miscalculation on the part of the driver would send the vehicle over the steep ledge and into a bottomless pit of snow. But Lauren had a feeling that impending danger did not keep them silent as much as their private worlds of thought. She herself was trying to put the two Jessicas together into a single personality—to get used to the idea of her being a widow, of her uncle's having been married *(Why hadn't Nella told her?)*, and of Troy's plan to include her in his missionary work. She felt a thrill of excitement and challenge. The day had gone wonderfully well.

At the door of the inn, Jessica said, "We must peel off this heavy clothing before we thaw—not just the parkas, but *all* of it. Don't be shy if there's anybody around."

Hopefully there wouldn't be. But there was. The Petrovs sat holding hands and looking idly out the window of the great room, causing Lauren to wonder fleetingly just how long the honeymoon was to continue. Then she spotted Troy and saw the look of concern on his face.

"I said shed 'em!" Jessica, all nurse, hissed. "Do you want to come down with pneumonia?"

And before Lauren could grasp what was happening, the other girl was practically tearing away her clothes before taking care of herself. Languidly she felt the heat touch her face and then what must have been her near-nude body. One part of her wanted to flee in embarrassment. The other wanted to crumple cozily and drift off to sleep. Somebody was wrapping a heavy towel around her body. Somebody else was chafing her wrists.

"You'll be all right," Troy whispered. "It's a natural reaction. But, oh, my darling, I was worried."

Dimly she realized that he shouldn't be using the words. But she was too deliciously tired to care. Maybe she should sleep.

"On your feet!" Jessica spoke with authority. "Want to walk on your own or have a snort of the hooch?"

"I'll walk," she said feebly.

Fortunately her strength came back quickly, and she

would have picked up her wet clothing except that Nella raised a protesting hand. "Behave yourself! Tuk's gone for your robe and then you're to hit the tub."

Nella gave the clothes a shake on the newspapers that she had spread at the storm doors, then took them piece-by-piece to dry beside the great fireplace.

And then came the incident which completely startled everybody in the room. As Nella shook the last wet garment, which happened to be the blue parka that Lauren had borrowed from her aunt, there was a little tinkle like the dropping of a silver coin.

"Something from your pocket—" Nella began. But before she could continue, Jessica, clad only in a heavy towel, sprang forward and tore it from her hand.

"It was Lauren's—" Nella began again. Jessica ignored the words, jerked her robe from a hook in the closet, pulled it quickly over the towel draped around her body, and started for the hall.

"Jessica!" Dr. Piriot's voice was sharp, but it fell on deaf ears. The girl was gone. "*Now* who's being foolish?" The doctor said in despair.

"What was it, anyway?" Nella asked.

The others didn't know, they said, and then her eyes focused on Lauren. "What was it she took?"

"A ring," she said, and because Anna Petrov's eyes were burning into her own, she decided against explaining.

But the tranquility of the day was destroyed. Whatever she and Jessica had shared during the trip to the Eskimo village was gone. Jessica's hatred and suspicion were back—only now Lauren realized that it was more far-reaching than jealousy. What could it be?

Chapter Seven

Lauren felt warm and relaxed after a warm bath, but she had a sensation of tingling in her hands and feet. Either it was new or she simply had never noticed it before. Thinking it was the orchid sweater-top she had chosen to wear with the long, pleated black skirt that caused her fingers to look purple, she changed into a white angora sweater with a cowl neckline even though it meant changing her shade of lipstick. She was glad of the change. It was warmer and more becoming.

"Feeling better?" Troy asked, his dark eyes showing the usual concern when she entered the dining room and sat down at his left.

"Much," she smiled, picking up her salad fork.

Immediately she laid it down. "Wow!" she said to Dr. Piriot, who sat at her left. "Tuk must have forgotten to thaw the silverware."

He smiled and then said casually, "I'll check you over tomorrow morning."

Probably routine, Lauren supposed, but wondered why his eyes remained on her right hand. True, the fingers were white, but the fork had been cold. Someone spoke to her and she forgot the incident.

Over raisin pie and coffee, Nella announced that a newcomer would be arriving during the week. The news brought a series of questions. Who? What was his business? It was a *man,* didn't she say? And would there be plenty of space...supplies?

"Wait, whoa, *whoa!* A man, yes, and as to his occupation," she shrugged, "something to do with the government. Rooms and supplies are my department, but we can accommodate several more people without any discomfort on anybody's part. So, *salute!*"

When Nella lifted her cup, the others lifted theirs. *"Salute!"*

Lauren smiled, remembering their toast to her—a traditional welcome, her aunt had explained. But the smile froze on her face when she looked across the table and saw Jessica's lifted cup. For there on the forefinger of her right hand was a ring which was a perfect twin to the gold signet ring that Ty wore. Biting her lip in concentration, Lauren tried to remember if he wore the ring on the right or left hand. The left! She recalled his having said that he was ambidextrous and the ring told him which hand to use in an introduction. He had said it lightly but in a way which discouraged another question. So she never knew why he chose the forefinger for a piece of jewelry.

Lauren's heart began to pound unmercifully. Something was wrong here. *Definitely* wrong. The ring Jessica wore had to be the one Lauren had picked up in the hall and never had an opportunity to examine.

It was understandable that she would wish to have it back, but nothing else made sense.

When I look up, she thought with her eyes fixed unseeingly on her dessert dish, *Jessica will be staring at me with a mixture of hatred and triumph.* But she was wrong. Jessica's ice-blue eyes were locked mockingly with someone else's.

Lauren tried to look casual as she let her eyes wander down the table to where she thought Jessica's gaze was fixed. *Anna!* Anna Petrov, her eyes blazing dangerously and then narrowing to peculiar, feline slits, was glaring back at the other girl.

Was nobody else witnessing the staring match? Apparently not. And she *couldn't* be imagining it. It was just that the others, like the characters in a soap opera when the camera is aimed at another actor, were totally uninvolved in the scenario.

The furious beating of her heart slowed, leaving Lauren shaken and weak. She tried to inhale deeply, but the breath lodged in her throat.

"Your color's too high. You look feverish." Dr. Piriot pushed back his chair. "I prescribe bed this minute with a hotwater bottle. I think I'll run a series of tests," he added as if thinking to himself.

Toward the end of the week, Dr. Piriot told Lauren that she could resume normal activities *indoors*. "And one violation, young lady, and it's right back to bed."

"I feel fine," Lauren protested. "It was just the cold and—"

When she did not continue, he looked at her closely. "It's just as I thought. Nobody has suggested to you that you have Raynaud's disease?"

Lauren shook her head. "I never heard of it."

"Most people haven't, so there's too little research on it for any real treatment. It's a rather rare circulatory disorder."

Lauren felt herself stiffen. It was incredible that she had anything wrong. "There must be some mistake."

"There's no mistake. You'll need to change your lifestyle."

"In what ways? Is this something I've recently contracted?"

"Congenital in your case. And, as to the changes I spoke of, no tobacco or—"

"Alcohol," Lauren supplied, hoping her voice did not betray her growing apprehension.

Dr. Piriot's heavy brows knitted, "I wasn't going to say alcohol and I know that you don't smoke. You will need to restrict yourself on coffee or any other caffeine. And avoid stress—"

Lauren sucked in her breath and interrupted, "Are you saying this is serious, Dr. Piriot?" The pounding had returned, and it was hard to get the words out.

"I dislike that word. The disease itself is not as 'serious' as the complications might be."

"Which are?"

He studied her face, fingered his pipe nervously, and seemed to discard the idea of lighting it. "That's another thing—try to avoid all others who smoke. I don't want you inhaling even secondhand!"

"The complications," Lauren's voice was a whisper.

"Lowered resistance to infections. Further breakdown in circulation. Possible gangrene in the extremities—but, come now, these we can prevent!"

He seemed to read her question, although her voice failed her.

"Let's be blunt, Lauren. You'll have to get back into a warm, dry climate—the sooner the better."

Lauren burst into tears as unexpected to herself as to Dr. Piriot. "I'm not ready for another decision—I was hoping to get my life straightened—and now—"

He put a warm, fatherly arm around her as if she were a small child. "I've upset you unnecessarily, my child. It needn't be today or tomorrow—and you loved California."

She adored California...the salt air...the sandy beaches...the hot sun beating down on her bare back...the pines...the poppies...and *Eric!* But she wasn't ready to return to where a part of her heart lingered. Not until she was a whole person, and certainly not in a state of shock like this...

It was good to have Nella tuck her in like a mother hen and to snuggle beneath the eiderdown softness of the added comforter, but sleep refused to come. In an effort to postpone thinking about the diagnosis that Dr. Piriot had made, with its implications and ultimatums, Lauren tried to recall some of the pleasant and surprising revelations of the day's drive to Kakalota. But it was impossible to think of anything except the strangeness of the evening.

Surely there was a logical explanation for the ring Jessica wore. Or was there? Come to think about it, life here had brought a series of mysteries that she had a feeling tied together in some as-yet unexplainable way.

At first her feverish thoughts concentrated on Jessica, whose resentment of her presence she had accepted until now as being jealousy. But now she wondered at the about-face swings of the girl's attitude...resentful before, but today almost friendly... then tonight the swingback to a certain mystifying behavior that Lauren remembered but could hardly put her finger upon.

Restlessly she turned over and tried to control her thoughts. But the nagging question came back: *What had Jessica's grab for the ring triggered in her memory?* When the answer came, Lauren sat straight up in bed. The letter! Of course, the little tug-of-war scene of Jessica and Anna's grappling over the letter.

Grasping her knees and shivering, Lauren sat in her egg-shaped position, trying desperately to get hold of some vague connection that she seemed to remember in flashbacks that refused to stay in focus long enough to be pieced together. Letter...letter..."envelope...just stamp and mail...in Seattle..."

Ty's voice! That was it. The letter she had mailed for him had been to Jessica. Only it wasn't Jessica who received it, her tired mind recalled. It was Anna Petrov.

"I'm going to have to talk to someone about this," she said aloud to the empty room. But which ones could she trust? Alarmed at her thinking, Lauren slid back under the covers and realized then that she was chilled to the bone.

When her teeth stopped chattering, Lauren prayed for a long time, asking God to guide her through this new crisis in her life. "I've felt so deeply that You brought me here for a purpose, Lord, and that I was fulfilling it. Should I stop now just because of this—this disease I'm supposed to have? I need Your help and guidance as never before. And, Lord, if these things I'm seeing here have any significance, show me how to handle whatever it is You are saying. I—I feel so helpless—''

Lauren cried then, letting the tears flow blessedly down her cheeks. When the great release was done, she carefully turned her pillow and prayed for Mother, Eric, and Ty—unaware that she had arranged any sort of priority—and then all the guests here and their missions...the children with whom she worked...and Eric again...

Finally she drifted into a pale, gray sleep in which she tracked through unfamiliar woods in search of an orienting landmark. The scene shifted. She and Mother were doing needlepoint on a giant canvas. Mother thought it was beautiful, but Lauren had the uneasy feeling that too many threads were being pulled loose, too many corners were unraveling. Yet she and Mother were ''winners,'' and some faceless audience applauded...only she, a wan victor, was too weak to walk the short distance and accept her prize...

There's someone at my door...

Had she said it in her dream? Lauren awoke in the half-light of dawn aware that she was frightened and cold. Quickly she switched on the bedside light and reached for the heavy pink robe and fleecy slippers. The furnace must have gone off, and the way the wind was howling, another Arctic blizzard must have struck.

For a moment she was tempted to brave the cold of the hall and go to her aunt's room. She remembered then that there were extra blankets in the hall closet. Maybe there was a heating pad too. The doctor and Jessica kept some of their first aid supplies there. That would be better than disturbing Nella.

Shivering, she padded noiselessly across the few

steps to the closet, holding her flashlight directly in front of her and carefully keeping the beam lowered to avoid the possibility of awakening Jessica, the only other occupant in this triad between doors.

The door seemed reluctant to open, and for a moment Lauren thought it was locked. When it yielded to stronger pressure, it burst open with a loud creak of the hinges. Startled, Lauren dropped the flashlight, but it was not the minor accident that caused her heart to start as if hit by a volt of electricity. It was the overpowering odor of oranges!

For a moment her mind refused to function, and her heart, after its initial shock, seemed to stop beating completely. What could oranges be doing here—here in Alaska, where fresh fruit was almost unheard of—and why in a closet?

With numb hands she felt for the flashlight, located it, and switched it back on, grateful that it had not been ruined in the fall. It took a minute or so to pull away the blankets and heavy garments that someone had used to hide the crate in which the oranges had been shipped. Once released, the dream-sweet odor engulfed her.

It was hard to make her near-paralyzed hands work, but Lauren was determined to find the label on the crate. It was no surprise that her name was printed on the outside covering and no surprise either that the return address bore Eric's name. Had she dreamed that part too? Or maybe in her subconscious mind she had suspected something all along when she kept smelling the fruit each time her door opened. The oranges would be frozen in spite of their heavy content of sugar. Nothing could escape in this temperature...

Glancing over her shoulder, Lauren saw a crack of light beneath Jessica's door. That was no surprise either. But the girl wasn't going to get away with this! Near panic, she tore at the thin label bearing Eric's address, finally succeeding in getting what she hoped was enough to put her in touch with him. Then, fearing hypothermia, she ran to Nella's room and rapped on the door with knuckles she no longer could feel.

"Let me in, Aunt Nella—*Oh, dear God, help me,*" she sobbed.

Two days later Lauren sat propped up on one of the couches in the front room of the inn, her pale face scarcely visible above the worktable, the ancient manual typewriter, and a mountain of books. Through little porthole-shaped spots in the east window she could see the faint white ribbon of road that climbed toward a still-higher line of snow-piled mountains leading to the village. Dr. Piriot, Jessica, and Troy had gone that direction this morning to check on damages left by the latest storm.

"You *will* follow the doctor's orders, baby?" After Lauren's reassurance that she had no choice, Nella had gone down the mountain road to pick up the mail, delayed three days by the blizzard. The evening would be a gala one. Everybody would be excited over the day's events, after having been imprisoned by the weather for two days. And Lauren could get herself dressed and join them for dinner. She closed her eyes for a prayer of thanksgiving before attacking her books and scribbled notes of research.

Dr. Piriot had been firm about what he considered the "ideal atmosphere for survival." He had smiled gravely at Lauren and Nella, the smile saying that he understood how difficult the taking of his advice would be. Too ill to argue that night, Lauren had nodded numbly—her thoughts divided feverishly between the mystery of the oranges and her misery. Misery won out and she had slept around the clock after the doctor brought her body heat back to normal and gave her a mild sedative—but not before she had extracted a promise from Dr. Piriot and her aunt.

"You won't tell the others?" Her voice had been pleading and desperate.

"Just that you're suffering from exposure," Dr. Piriot said.

"You weren't going to tell *me* either, were you?" Nella's voice was gently chiding.

When Lauren admitted she wasn't with a shake of her head, the doctor said gently, "Seems to me you're bent on keeping secrets, Miss Lauren Eldridge!"

"Seems to me I'm not the only one in this house—" Lauren had replied sleepily.

Her last clear memory as sleep took her head was the two of them looking at each other with primitive flushes of guilt on their faces...

Lauren chewed on the eraser of her pencil. In just a moment she would get back to the book outline, but not before she settled another matter in her mind. Wasn't there something else she remembered hazily? Suspended between two worlds, hadn't she heard Nella tell Dr. Piriot about the discovered oranges? In her own hysteria, Lauren had sobbed out the story between her aunt's frenzied call to the doctor and his arrival.

The memory shimmered a moment...dimmed tantalizingly, like the fadeout on a television screen just when the viewer is yearning to see more...and then came with sudden clarity!

Nella: "Jessica! Correct?"

Dr. Piriot: "Correct, but there's a reason, my dear Nella."

Nella: "No reason is good enough. Lauren will never forgive her."

Dr. Piriot: "She will when she knows the circumstances."

Nella: "Andy, tell me so *I* can understand. We have no secrets from each other—just from the others."

Dr. Piriot (regretfully): "I can't, dear Nella, I can't. But some day—some day soon—you will know..."

The scenario faded and today's world came back into focus. *Enough of these fantasies, Lauren,* she told herself. Why, soon she would be creating heavy dramas and disasters! And, goodness knows, there were enough of those around in the natural world.

Determinedly she reached to unearth the partially finished outline of *Amen to the Altar* from beneath the pile of books. They tottered under her touch. With one hand holding onto the couch, Lauren tried to steady the stack with her other. But a dozen books skittered to the rug, scattering pages of jotted notes as they fell.

Straining in her awkward position, Lauren tried to recover the notes and put them back in the right places as bookmarks. Then a sheaf of her near-illegible scribblings fluttered from the Bible. "My darling Eric: The oranges were the words you have never spoken, *I love you*..." The words were crossed out lightly. The next message began: "Darling One: Who cares what rules society says we must follow?..." Lauren read on, each word a knife in her heart: "Eric, my one true love..."

"Eric, I love you, not as I, your sister, should..." and finally, *"Oh, Eric, what can we do?"*

"I should have mailed one of them, written in my delirium though they may have been," Lauren said aloud, sadness and helplessness tugging at her heart. "They were the truth poured from my heart, soul, and body as God would have me tell it. I've asked Him for an answer, Eric, and He gave it. It's here on these scraps of paper that I didn't have the courage to mail!"

If Eric were here, he would know what to do about her physical problem. He would know, too, what was to be done about the Eskimo children who had come to depend upon her...and the mysteries that now Lauren was sure were no figments of her imagination...yes, he would know how to solve the mysteries, too...

The practical Lauren took over as Lauren-the-Dreamer fled. She knew with a twinge of bitterness that she had done the right thing in sending the letter she finally wrote when her fever had passed. By now it was on its way to the Mexican address she had scratched from the crate of frozen oranges.

It was a good letter, a proper letter, one written in the same style that baffled Ty, her parents, and her friends—everybody except Eric. Eric alone understood her, maybe better than she understood herself. He did not find her peculiar or think that her moral and spiritual values were "quaint and old-world, completely out of tune with the 1980s"...Now where did that phrase come from? Oh, from Ty! *Ty!* The man who wanted to marry her and about whom she should be thinking. *No,* she thought determinedly, *I will not think of him or about what might have been with Eric. I will concentrate on my book!*

Not wishing to drop the scribbled notes to Eric in
the wastebasket in case someone should pick them up,
she carefully folded them into tiny squares and returned them to her Bible. Eric would appreciate her
description of the countryside and its people. He would
enjoy the lightly written description of her "ups and
downs" to seek out the houses which often were so
buried in the snow that they were little easier to see
than the moraines themselves. "You should see this
twilight zone, Eric," she had concluded. "Would you
believe that the stars are visible even in the daytime?
And at night they are so close you can touch them—a
million light-years away, I guess, but it's easy to believe
they really are starfish! Come and we'll find out."

Eric would wonder about her book. Purposely she
had made no mention of it, because she would have
been unable to report any progress. Well, the next time
would be different...if there was to be a next time...

"And, dear God, let there be," she prayed aloud.
Peace came then. It was as if God had answered immediately instead of waiting: "There will be!"

Feeling alive and vibrant, she wrote with inspired
words that were not hers at all:

> Our view of marriage is too low. We need
> to lift our eyes to a Higher Court where
> presides the Judge whose pattern is laid out
> in the Book of Law by which we must cut
> our patterns. These patterns are, old-
> fashioned though it may sound, heart-
> shaped things called love, the only valid
> reason for entering into a marital relation-
> ship. This love knows no limits, no condi-

tions, and no termination. Under a micro-
scope, this love could not be seen. It is a
feeling. But feelings manifest themselves
into action, decisions, and commitments.
By these we know the "feeling" is there.
How unconditional and everlasting is this
love? Only God's love has both those qualities. But how close can an earthly love
come to achieving a portion of His stan-
dards? Read what 1000 married women responding to a 50-question questionnaire
have to say regarding the importance of
faith in God to the vows they take at the
altar...

Exhausted and happy, Lauren laid her pencil down.
It would be a good book. God was her Co-author!

Chapter Eight

Late in the afternoon, Lauren, elated over the progress she had made with her manuscript, put away her working materials, tidied the front room, and felt wonderful. The doctor surely must be wrong. It was impossible to have some obscure disease, whatever he had called it, and feel this fit. She reached her decision: Leaving here was out of the question until the year was up. Everything was shaping up remarkably well, and while she had reached no other decisions, Lauren had a strong feeling that the answers would come. Besides, there were too many loose ends to tie up...

One of these days I will seek the opinion of a specialist, Lauren promised herself on the way to the bathroom. But for now things could go on as always. Lauren hummed as she poured bubble bath into the tub and watched the froth of perfumed bubbles build up invitingly like billows of cumulous clouds.

Wiping the steam from the bathroom mirror as she

toweled herself dry, Lauren saw that the humidity had caused her hair to go its own way to form a million ringlets. On impulse she pulled the damp, ash-gold cascade on top of her head and secured it experimentally with pins. "Why, you look regal, Miss Eldridge," she told her reflection playfully. Then, giggling, she patted a few stray curls dry against her temples before slipping into the only really dressy gown she had brought along. The princess-like fuschia velvet was stunning. A string of pearls? Yes, her choker. And a touch—just a *touch*—of French perfume that Ty had given her for her birthday last summer. Wishing that she need not wear a wrap, Lauren pulled the black angora stole about her shoulders and made her way hurriedly through the halls toward the front room, where most of the others would have gathered.

At the door she paused, sensing somehow that something was wrong. How ridiculous! She squared her shoulders, unaware of what a beautiful picture she would make framed by the doorway with the firelight reflecting on her pale hair, and opened the door.

In the split second before the group acknowledged her presence, Lauren's eyes saw—as in one of her fantasies—that the new guest had arrived. The stranger who "had something to do with the government." But the man was no stranger. And if he had anything to do with the government, it was news to Lauren. *Ty... How could it be?*

Forever afterward Lauren would remember the scene that followed only as indistinctly as she remembered confusing dreams. She stood a lifetime, it seemed, like a lifeless doll in the presence of a total stranger while a roomful of spectators waited for action.

Ty's compelling eyes were fastened on her admiringly, hungrily. But she kept her gaze averted. *If I look at him, I will melt into a mass of nothingness, having no will of my own,* her mind said in that fleeting second. The eyes she could control, but not the wild fluttering of her heart. With a little gasp for breath that the others undoubtedly interpreted as joy, Lauren's hand went shakily to the bosom of her velvet gown in an effort to control her heart.

"Surprise!" the group chorused. "Look at her face!" someone said.

Lauren realized then that they had been awaiting her arrival. But how did they know? Surely Nella wouldn't have—

"Well, aren't you going to greet Mr. Valdez?" Above the loud drumming of her heart Lauren recognized Jessica's voice. Directing her words to Lauren, she added quickly, "Ty—Mr. Valdez—has told us your secret!"

Before Lauren could regain her composure, Ty had crossed the room in what seemed to be one graceful stride. It was all happening quickly, but Lauren's eyes had gone slow-motion. The room whirled muzzily. The dizziness increased and she swayed on her feet.

Ty caught her by the shoulders, "Hold on to me."

He took her arms and put them on his shoulders. To save herself from dropping to the floor, there was little recourse but to clasp her hands behind his head and lean against him.

"Please, Ty—please—" she whispered, a protest he chose to misinterpret.

Ty's grasp tightened. "Glad to oblige!" he whispered back.

Then, to her astonishment, he swung her up into his arms and turned to face the group. "My new friends," he said with mock formality, "Meet the future Mrs. Tyrone Valdez!"

The group—and Lauren was uncertain who all was witnessing her embarrassment and frustration—applauded. "Bravo! Bravo!"

Lauren struggled to free herself while Ty shamelessly removed the pins from her hair and let the cascade of curls tumble down around her face. Running his fingers through it intimately, Ty set her gently on her feet. With his right arm still firmly around her waist, he guided her to the nearest couch.

"I fear the surprise has been too much for her. Are you all right, my love?"

"Quite," she murmured, wondering what her friends here must be thinking. In an effort to maintain her dignity, Lauren asked—as one would address a total stranger—"Did you have a smooth flight?"

"Smooth? From Paris to Alaska? One could hardly expect that in midwinter. It was rough, slow—and *lonely!*"

There was a little ripple of polite laughter as he reached to take her hand. Wishing Ty would show more restraint and yet not wanting to arouse more curiosity than she felt his greeting had aroused already, Lauren concentrated on his hands. She had always admired their sensitivity, their slender power to reach out and take. *Take!* That was the word. The hands, like their owner, were *takers!* And I, her mind rushed on as if in sudden revelation, am a *giver*—but something interrupted her thoughts at that point. On Ty's index finger was the ring she remembered so vividly. It occurred to her then that probably Ty had sent her the twin ring and somehow Jessica had intercepted it as she had intercepted the oranges. That must be the answer.

Involuntarily her eyes sought his. She must explain at the first opportunity, ask forgiveness, and try to reestablish their former relationship.

But his next words shattered that hope. "If it bothers you that I choose to wear jewelry, I can remove the ring."

The words, lightly spoken, were somehow mocking. Lauren was glad that the others had picked up the conversation and were not concentrating on her and Ty. No denying that there was a lot for the two of them to unriddle and see what, if anything, remained. But not with an audience. Her cheeks burned with the memory of the episode they had witnessed a few minutes earlier. All she cared about now was that the remainder of the evening go without another embarrassing incident.

Resolutely trying to put the ring out of her mind, Lauren skirted Ty's comment. "I wish you'd written," she said instead.

"So you could shoo the new men in your life away before my arrival?" he whispered against her ear.

At that untimely moment Troy entered the room. "Our new guest!" His greeting was warm. "You must—you *have* to be—Eric."

Ty stood to accept Father Troy's extended hand of welcome. "Tyrone Valdez," he corrected with his usual social grace. "Were you expecting someone else?"

Troy's dark eyes sought Lauren's in apology. "No—not that I am aware. Forgive my mistake—"

But his stumbling told Ty what he wished to know. In the flickering firelight his face was in half-shadow, but Lauren saw his eyes fixed upon her. *Eric*, they said. A statement. Not a question.

There was a flurry of introductions. Then, to Lauren's immense relief, Tuk announced dinner.

Lauren was scarcely aware of the flow of conversation around her. She felt too weary to listen or to enter in. Ty mentioned his work, she remembered later—something about some government lands—wastelands, uninhabited, but where they were or what else he said she had missed.

Only once did he direct conversation to her. The others were discussing the damages of the recent storm when Ty leaned down to whisper, *"Eric*. My secret rival. But then, no matter what I have chosen to believe, none of us is perfect, my dear Lauren."

Without a word, determined to preserve the rest of the evening if possible, Lauren turned away. It was then that her eyes came in direct contact with Jessica's. Try as she would, it was impossible to read the expression in the other girl's eyes. It was as if she were trying to communicate something, and then the look changed as the cool, blue eyes shifted to meet Ty's. At that moment Jessica lifted her cup.

"Haven't we forgotten something?" she asked. "Sa-*lute!*"

The others lifted their cups and turned to Ty. Lauren's fingers fumbled and her cup clattered to the floor. Numbly she felt the hot coffee on her bare arms and watched the ugly brown stains penetrate the fuschia folds of the velvet gown. This couldn't be true...

On Jessica's right hand was the signet ring—twin to Ty's. The index finger of the girl's hand curled around the cup as if to make a public announcement of the two gems.

Dr. Piriot, Troy, and Nella hurried to hover over Lauren. Was she all right? How hot was the beverage? And didn't she think she should change?

As if in a trance, Lauren heard their questions and knew that her aunt was mopping the coffee from her lap. Maybe she answered. If so, had she told them that she was impervious to physical pain? They should be checking for internal injury. She was mortally wounded. *How can you,* her bleeding heart cried out, *concern yourselves with slightly reddened skin while the man who made such an open display of affection just moments ago is betraying me so openly.*

But they seemed totally unaware that Tyrone's eyes had locked with Jessica's. That *her* eyes were unashamedly inviting. And that *he* had lifted his ringed hand in a small salute bearing no resemblance to the toast of welcome. Was it recognition—or *familiarity?*

In humiliation, Lauren tried to look toward the wonderful people who were too busy with her own welfare to watch the hateful scene. They deserved a word of appreciation that she had failed to give. As she was about to turn away, however, her eyes moved past Anna and Ivan Petrov, then did a double take and returned. The exchange between Ty and Jessica was not lost upon the pair. The "newlyweds," who were hardly that anymore, having chosen to remain at this outpost for so long, were watching Ty and Jessica as a cat watches its prey. It was not a question of whether to pounce. Or how. It was only a matter of timing.

Lauren tried to speak, to thank Troy, who was bending over her so caringly, but tears choked at her throat.

Troy must have seen, for he took her gently by the shoulders. "Would you care to lie down?" he asked in the gentle voice he used for his parishioners.

Ty spoke at her elbow. "Is it spiritual comfort you are offering my fiancee', Reverend? Must she lie down for that?"

The voice was cold and expressionless. Even through her maze of mortification, Lauren saw that his face was very pale and that the long scar down the one cheek stood out against the pallor. Fear for Troy's safety momentarily replaced her embarrassment. *Oh, please, God—*

Troy, pale himself, made a gesture as if to speak. Then, to her immense relief, he bowed slightly and backed away in silence.

Lauren no longer cared what those around them heard or saw. Fury erased her fear. "What an ugly thing to say!" she said as quietly as possible. Then, shaking her head unbelievingly, she spoke in even softer tones, "How can you pretend to love me?"

Ty, back to his charming self, smiled for the benefit of those around the table who were exclaiming over Tuk's upside-down cake, and said almost inaudibly, "Forgive me. I was consumed by jealousy. I will apologize if it will make you happy."

Before Lauren could recover from her surprise, he continued, "It's just that I hadn't realized that the good rector entertained such tender notions. But then, obviously, the feelings are mutual, since you made no mention of our relationship."

Ty's words stung like an adder. All feeling seemed to drain from her body, leaving her cold and empty inside. *Relationship?* There *was* no relationship! There never could be. How could she have been so blind? How could she have—what was it that Troy Huguenot had said on her views of marriage? That one did not choose another person as if shopping and then "work" at loving that person? Surely he must be right. Love—the right kind of love—"came naturally."

"We must talk—" She must have said the words aloud, for Ty was answering as they moved back into the front room, "We have forever."

"It will not wait," she answered crisply.

Through a haze, Lauren bade the others good night, hoping that she said the right things. That Ty and Jessica exchanged a few words unobserved, they thought, made no difference to her now. What mattered was clearing away this terrible web into which she had fallen before she was consumed by her captor.

Nella must have sensed something, Lauren knew. She did remember her aunt's saying as she leaned to kiss Lauren's cheek, "No firm commitment, baby, promise? Until we can talk—"

Ty had claimed her hand then, but not before she nodded a silent promise.

"It's the ring, isn't it, my love?" Ty moved to sit on the couch nearest the dying fire and patted a place beside him once they were alone.

Lauren ignored his gesture. Walking to the fireplace, she poked at the fire before speaking. "It has nothing to do with the ring at this point," she said truthfully.

Lauren was unskilled at taking the initiative, particularly with men. She had paid little attention to women's liberation movements. Passive by nature—one of the things that caused everybody except Eric to think of her as a "peculiar adult"—she ordinarily would have waited for Ty to take the lead in this or any other conversation.

Tonight, however, she let her feelings out—carefully keeping her eyes on the dying embers of the once brightly-sparkling fire. Her feelings of uncertainty from the beginning...the need to be alone...his seeming agreement to her plan only to show up here without warning—how *had* he known just where to find her? When Ty did not answer, Lauren continued. "And tonight—oh, didn't you see what you were doing to me tonight?"

When tears caught at her throat, Lauren bit her lip, fighting for control. A certain sense of exhilaration rose within her. She had met a crisis, if only in conversation. It was good to have spoken up, and not to have held back. She wanted to hold onto that new courage—something she believed she had learned here in this strange new world.

When Lauren felt she was in control again, she dared glance at Ty—surprised that he had not spoken. What she saw in his face surprised her more and threatened to undermine her determination to have something settled before the two of them parted. He looked genuinely stricken.

"Why *did* you come here, Ty? Oh, please—" she lifted her hand to halt any more words about his being driven by the need to see her. "Tell me the truth—was it business, as you said? And, tell me," she said slowly as she recalled her Seattle mission, "what was the letter I mailed for you? It came here, you know."

"What I said was the truth. Business brought me here. The government is having my company look into a land development—something you would not understand. Come to think of it, my dear Lauren, you will never understand me—or even try to—will you?" It was hard for her to determine how sincere he was, and before she could respond he continued, "You can understand only your definition of godliness and piety. Maybe those qualities are what attracted me. You *are* different, you know, and utterly charming, but those qualities can become—well, tiresome, my dear. Come now," he lowered his voice, "can't you just relax, practice a little of this *believing* you cleave to, and be a bit more like the rest of us sinners?"

Confused and disappointed at the turn the conversation had taken, Lauren suddenly felt exhausted. When she failed to answer, Ty took it as a weakening on her part. Striding to where she stood, he touched her gently on the shoulder. "Look at me and deny that there is something between us!"

She stared at him blankly, wondering just what she did feel. There was so much that needed talking about.

"Don't fight it—" His arms reached out and encircled her, drawing her breathlessly near.

"No, no!" She struggled free, and—without bothering with her wrap—she fled to the sanctity of her bedroom. There, with her face buried in her hands, she wept until she could weep no more.

Dry-eyed and exhausted, she lay awake in the chill darkness. Only prayer could bring a healing balm to her troubled heart, but it was hard to pray for answers when she was unable to achieve enough orderliness of spirit to identify the questions.

"Forgive me, Lord," she thought disjointedly. "In a way which only You will understand, I feel guilty... guilty for coming here to resolve my problems instead

of staying to look after Mother...guilty for burden-
ing Nella...for somehow failing to see the symptoms
of this Raynaud's disease, getting the children to the
place where together You and I could have touched
their lives and then—then being unable to follow
through unless—unless You help me overcome the incurable. Only nothing is impossible with You...so how
can it be incurable, Lord? Just let me learn to deal with
it—if You can trust me again. You see, Lord, I know
I did not deal with a lot of things right tonight. Not
with Ty most of all. I took it for granted, Lord, that
he knew You. And now I knew what You knew all
along—I believed what I wanted to believe—"

Lauren paused when a dry sob caught in her throat,
then determinedly went on. "I could have helped
tonight—but I didn't. Ty poked fun at my faith. But
I did worse. I failed You when I did not try to set him
straight instead of letting my foolishness rule over
Your Spirit...worrying about what others were thinking...letting false pride make me deaf to Your voice.
I feel guilty about this—and about his being here—
just give me another chance..."

She drifted off into a troubled sleep. In that vast,
dark world of silence, Lauren did not dream. When she
awoke, she wished that dreams, however troubled, had
come. Psychologists said that dreams helped the dreamer
to resolve problems. Hers had not gone away...

But Ty had. Nella told her that he had dined early
and gone with Dr. Piriot and Jessica to the village.
Maybe they could talk, she and Nella? Yes, they
would, her aunt said eagerly—only to have Troy enter
and ask if she could spend some planning time with
him.

Chapter Nine

The talk with Troy went well. Unable to dismiss memories of the night before, Lauren was afraid that her thoughts would betray her or that he would refer to the evening. The ups and downs of all that had happened puzzled and repelled her, but to say she did not care for Ty? Everything went back to Ty. The ring... the letter...his wild behavior...Tyrone Valdez might be an adventurer—an absolute scoundrel. He had humiliated her. He had insulted Troy. He had shamelessly played up to Jessica. And yet—she flushed painfully with the memory—at the very end of the conversation she had been taken in by him again. How could she, Lauren asked herself in the reasoned light of the winter day, have deceived herself and mistaken his guile for the kind of tenderness that went with love? *But what does he want of me?*

Forcing further questions out of her mind, Lauren smiled at Father Troy, who busily laid out papers and notes in preparation for their planning session. She was grateful for his comforting presence. Unaware of her illness or of the churning inside her, Troy would put new direction and purpose to her days. It would have been so easy to become depressed, to simply lose interest in life. Every way she turned, there seemed to be unresolved problems, like a series of little moraines, rising one after the other, waiting to be climbed in a few easy strides. But beyond each lay another, each higher and steeper, each more insurmountable.

"I saw the mink you drew for Dr. Piriot," Troy said as he sat down beside her at the table.

"I'm afraid it wasn't much of a likeness—it was something I picked up from a travel folder."

"The likeness was clear enough to give me an idea, Lauren. You will be feeling up to resuming the newsletter soon, I gather?" When she nodded, Troy continued, "I want very much to usurp more of your time now that the doctor is requiring less of you."

"He told me. And before you ask," she smiled brightly, "the answer is yes. I want to resume working directly with the children."

"Excellent! Has anyone told you of the celebrations the villagers have come to make a part of the winter solstice—the potlash?"

Nobody had, and Lauren listened with keen interest as Troy described the tradition each family followed of making and erecting a totem pole bearing the family crest and whatever bits of history each wished to exhibit. A part of the potlash was the ceremonial feast which followed, a time for gift-giving.

"Like Christmas?" Lauren wondered.

Troy's eyes lit up with excitement. "Ah, my dear

Lauren, you are ahead of my lesson plans! What I wish to propose is the making of a Christian totem pole—one which depicts the birth of our Savior—"

"Oh, wonderful!" Lauren was caught up completely in his excitement. "We can sketch the drawings—the children can carve—"

"And what a glorious opportunity for us to go more deeply into the blessed meaning of Christ's birthday!"

"Do you suppose that the airport families would wish to join in?" Lauren asked.

"Oh, they do—there are dogsled races, folk dancing, all sorts of recreation. Fortunately, Kakalota is a dry section—no alcohol allowed in the vicinity—so it is safe and harmless for the children."

So engrossed were they in the planning that Lauren was unaware that noon had come and gone unnoticed until her stomach reminded her with a gnaw of emptiness. Reluctantly she excused herself and went in to tidy up for dinner. Soon the others would be back—Dr. Piriot, Jessica, and Ty from the village, plus Nella from the airport with the mail. With the thought came a sudden chill. What lay ahead for the evening—and for the days to come?

On the surface, dinner was a gala affair. Underneath, Lauren sensed the same undercurrent she felt inside herself. Desperately anxious that Ty should not mistake her moment of weakness last night as compliance with whatever plans he might have for himself and her, or, even worse, that he should make a similar scene, she strove to give the impression of warmth—at arm's length.

Ty, on the other hand, was unusually talkative, seeming to captivate the other diners with his wit and charm. Occasionally he turned an attentive gaze in Lauren's direction as if it were expected. Otherwise he was remote, treating her with a strange and formal politeness.

As Ty related an amusing account of his visit with the owner of the Kakalota Trading Post, Lauren studied the reactions of those around her. Nella and the doctor seemed to look at each other frequently—more frequently than usual? Lauren dismissed the thought. Actually, she had never paid that much attention to the two of them together. Jessica, as Lauren would have expected, laughed with frequent amusement, interrupting now and then to embroider Ty's account. Nothing unusual about the group so far. But the Petrovs were another matter. Usually withdrawn, seeming to prefer each other's company without intrusion, tonight they hung onto every word that both Ty and Jessica were saying.

Feeling that she herself was being observed, Lauren turned to meet the level gaze of Troy. There was nothing personal in his eyes. Just a wordless message that he too was watching and finding something irregular.

"Tell me, Mr. Valdez," Anna Petrov said in her low, throaty rasp that Lauren found both fascinating and irritating, "do you plan to stay on for awhile?"

"Oh, yes, quite some time, providing our hostess can provide lodging?" At Nella's nod, Ty continued, "It will take several weeks at least to—shall we say—wind up my *affairs?*"

Knowing that her face was flushed with embarrassment, Lauren nevertheless turned to look at Ty. His overemphasis on the last word had warned of more to come. *Not tonight, please!* her eyes pleaded.

To her relief, Ty entered into a conversation, led by Anna and Ivan, about fishing, cross-country skiing, wild-game hunting, and casino life in some of the cities. "But what about transportation?" he asked Ivan.

"Helicopter, perhaps? Or we could travel by air. There are a good many bush plane pilots whose services we could engage."

Lauren saw a flicker in the depths of Ty's dark eyes. "How far into the interior do these bush pilots fly? And what is their load capacity—for gear, you know?" he asked Ivan.

Lauren was so surprised by Ty's high interest that she failed to hear the answers. What could this information have to do with the investigation of government lands? Didn't he know where the lands were?

With that question all the other questions surfaced again in her mind. It was then that she remembered the mystery of the ring and, glancing at Jessica's hand, she saw that the turquoise gem was missing. The fact that Ty continued to wear his ring told her nothing.

In the days that followed, Ty was seldom at the inn. When he was there, he spent much of his time poring over maps spread out on the library table. With his usual magnetism, he drew the other guests' attention to his activities. Lauren felt a sense of relief. That way they hardly seemed to notice that she resumed the trips to Kakalota. Undetected, she was neither questioned nor scolded. Her mother had sent the promised packet of completed questionnaires, but the project at the village occupied so much time that Lauren found no time to resume work on her book. Nella had come down with a cold and Dr. Piriot confined her to bed and advised the others to avoid contact. "Especially you," he said in a little aside to Lauren.

"Those phrases seem to be the password around here," she said soberly. The doctor looked puzzled, but she did not continue. The words had slipped out and did not concern him. She needed to talk with Nella and with Ty. Secretly, however, Lauren was pleased about the delay of both conversations. They would somehow tie together, she was certain. She wondered—actually *feared*, perhaps unreasonably—what her aunt might reveal. Secrets had been a way of life with her for so many years that the very word carried an ominous threat.

And, as for Ty, she was no closer to a resolution of her feelings toward him than she had been. Actually, her emotions were more complicated. Hating herself for her suspicions, Lauren felt sure in her heart that he was involved in something illegal, dangerous, or both. But, try as she would, there was no dismissing a certain responsibility she felt for his being here, as well as a strong desire to make good her promise to God that she would find a way to approach him without sounding, as he had said, "filled with godliness and piety," qualities he abhorred. Maybe timing was as important as her aunt had declared.

Lauren found it increasingly difficult to sleep. She lay wakeful and restless as she wrestled with pieces of this strange puzzle, wondering where each person who made up its mysterious design fit, or if most of them fit in at all. "If only I could confide in somebody, Lord," she whispered over and over, "but I don't know my friends from my enemies."

On one of those nights Lauren was disturbed by the

distant howling of the timber wolves. Their lonely, hungry cries sent chills up and down her spine. She listened, her fingers gripping the coverlet tightly. The pack seemed to come close to the inn, then gradually their plaintive cries grew more distant. The numbness that Lauren had experienced more and more of late increased in her fingers, and she was massaging them beneath the covers as Dr. Piriot had directed when a lone wolf—totally unnatural in sound—seemed to echo from beneath her very window, causing the blood to curdle in her veins.

Something was wrong. Instinctively wrapping a heavy robe around her body, Lauren crept to the window, blew her breath on the pane, and with the sleeve of her robe cleared a small section of the glass.

The nightlight on the crest of the bright snow outlined a shadowy figure slinking between two drifts that had been cleared for a passageway. But the shadow was not that of an animal. It was a man!

At another low cry, there was a whisper of footsteps in the hall. Hardly breathing, Lauren waited. The wolflike call had been a signal. But what did it mean?

The answer came quickly. Another figure emerged from the front door of the inn and joined the one standing in the shadows. The two people, one of which most certainly was a woman, appeared to argue. Then, as if the matter were settled, the two of them moved down the tunneled walk together. Just as they reached a slight bend between the drifts, the man turned to glance furtively over his shoulder. Caught in the cone of light, the face was easily recognizable—the darkness of the skin and eyes against the brilliant white of the background, the scar standing out angrily. *Ty!*

Shivering, Lauren moved from the window, eased her door open a crack, and adjusted her eyes to the darkness of the hall. Sure enough, the door to Jessica's room stood open.

In an irrational moment of hurt and anger, Lauren was tempted to enter the other girl's room and look for evidence of what was going on. That it had to do with something more than a romantic involvement was evident. Nobody of sound mind would go out into the dangers of the frozen night in order to be alone.

A sudden whisper of repeated footsteps broke the silence. Jessica, bundled in her parka and mukluks, whisked almost inaudibly through the door of her room. Immobilized, Lauren listened to the bolt slip into place. *If I had the strength, I would break down that door, force my way inside, and demand some answers,* she thought numbly. Then, almost unaware of her motions, she crawled back into bed where she lay in a state of shock—cold and unfeeling.

Sometime during the rest of the long, sleepless night, there came the sound of a motor, muffled and low. The little hum was gone as quickly as it came. Mission accomplished—whatever it was. There was nothing Lauren could do but wait for the coming of a gray morning...and wonder if Ty would return safely ...or if she cared...

To Lauren's complete amazement, Ty—looking fit and rested—appeared for an early breakfast. In an effort to hide her surprise, Lauren searched for words.

"It's good to see you, Ty," she murmured.

"And why would you not expect my presence, my love?"

Ty's voice was teasing, but his words caused Lauren

to glance at him quickly. Was there a hidden meaning to what he asked?

His smile was unreadable. "I—I don't know," she stumbled. "I mean, I thought maybe you were away or—" she hurried on, "that you would spend some time with me if—"

The words sounded foolish to her own ears. Even as she listened to Ty, one part of her was hoping that Jessica was not hearing her grope.

"That I would spend some time with you if *I* had the time?" Ty finished for her. "Indeed I would! And I *will* as soon as my work here is finished. Last night I was mapping out the areas—would you believe that some of them are as yet unexplored?"

"No," Lauren said slowly, and then with more conviction, "not by white men, maybe. But I doubt that any section is totally foreign to the natives."

"And who, my dear, are the 'natives'?"

"The Indians, Tlingit and Haida, then the Aleuts, Athabascans, Eskimos—are you listening to me?" Lauren asked when she saw his hint of a smile. "Do you find me amusing?"

"Oh, I do!" Ty's smile—almost tender in his amusement—was disarming.

Turning away, she continued, "With all the skilled sailors and navigators coupled with nomads who followed the migrating caribou, I find it hard to believe that any of the territories are truly unexplored."

Ty's laugh was deep, low, and compelling—one of the qualities that commanded the attention of women. Lauren was aware that its sound drew Jessica's and Anna's gazes their direction. She was aware, too, that as usual the conversation had gone out on a tangent.

Neither fact bothered her, for she was suddenly sure that in Ty's words lay a key to his presence here and the other mysteries surrounding it.

She waited for him to go on. When he resumed, it was to say, "You are well-versed for one so new here. You are a better-informed tourist than they were."

"They?"

"The 'natives,' as you choose to call them. That's what they were, you know. Just tourists."

Something churned inside Lauren. "You speak as if you don't like them," she said in a voice she kept carefully low and controlled.

Ty accepted a second cup of coffee, thanked Tuk, and resumed his attitude of charmed amusement. "Like them?" He shrugged and began to stir his coffee with unconcern. "They're no better and no worse than the rest of humanity, I guess—except for the elect."

Lauren chose to ignore his meaningful look at Troy Huguenot. "Ty," she said, hoping to catch him off guard, "will you come to church with me Sunday?"

At the unexpected question, Ty was speechless, a reaction she had never seen in him before. The moment passed quickly and he was back in the usual role.

"I thank you for your interest in my soul, my love. But, you see, I have other plans. I am going up the river in a charter plane with the Petrovs as guides. As a matter of fact, I think it would be a great idea if you came along. Can you ski?"

Lauren nodded. It had been some time since her family and Eric's had gone to Mount Palomar—back in the days when nothing had ended her childhood world, when her heart was whole, and when her body was whole too. Dr. Piriot had said she could never ski again...and she wouldn't risk it until she had another diagnosis...

"Lauren?" Ty was waiting for an answer.

She jumped. "I'm sorry. I was just considering. I—I don't ski well. Would I be in your way—?"

"I won't be skiing," he said smoothly. "I would have arranged to have you accompany Anna and Ivan."

Throughout the conversation, Lauren realized now, she had entertained the foolish hope that she was exaggerating the circumstances of Ty's presence here. How foolish!

Impetuously she said, "Ty, when can we get together?"

He squeezed her hand beneath the white table cloth. "*Any* time!"

Lauren felt her face flush. "I mean to talk," she said.

"Well now," his voice was low and intimate, "we should talk before the wedding, shouldn't we? By the way, I will go to church with you *that* day."

His words were intended to amuse her. Instead, she was incredibly angry. "We *have* no plans, Ty," she whispered, careful that her voice was well out of hearing range of the others. "I need to know exactly what it is you want of me!"

Lauren saw that once again her words had shaken him. She had struck something inside Ty which he dared not have discovered...

When Dr. Piriot declared Nella out of "quarantine," she immediately suggested a private talk with Lauren. Once they were comfortably seated alone in the front room, Nella waved any inquiries about her own health and asked, "Are you taking care, baby? It breaks my heart to ask this—but have you given any thought to getting back home?"

"This *is* home," Lauren protested. And in a very real sense it was true.

Her aunt shook her head sadly. "No. Not really. I understand what you're saying, and you've done wonders. But Alaska must not become a hiding-out place."

The idea was new to Lauren, but her aunt's advice made sense—in all ways except for the new developments. She wondered how much Nella knew. Then, encouraged by a look of concern in her aunt's face, Lauren poured out the entire story beginning with the letter Ty had instructed her to mail and ending with the news that he and the Petrovs had gone into the interior.

Nella remained quiet for so long after the story that Lauren wondered if she had heard it all. At length she spoke. "Do you think there's a connection in all this—the letter, the ring, the Petrovs, and Jessica?"

Lauren admitted that she did. "Even the oranges fit in somewhere, but I can't figure out how."

"But you can't think Eric is involved!"

"Oh, no, not Eric—it's more something to do with my mail." Lauren stopped short then, for the idea she was about to share was new to her. "Nella," she said slowly, "do you suppose Jessica could have been checking on *me?* That I'm a suspect in whatever's going on? No," she dismissed the idea herself, "it couldn't be that—not with her meeting Ty as she did in that midnight rendezvous."

"We'd better be cautious until we know who's involved," Nella said. "Not the friar, most certainly—and not Andy—Dr. Piriot."

"No, neither of them." Lauren was as positive as her aunt. "But you do see why I can't leave here now—and, oh, you should see how our project's coming along for the potlatch!"

"I know," Nella said quietly. "You and Father Troy have a good thing going."

"Not like that!"

"Not like anything. Just a good thing, period. But, Lauren, nothing you have told me is as important as your life."

"Oh, come now! What I have is not that serious. And I'm taking care. I'm putting on so many extra pairs of long johns that I can hardly bend over to pick up something the children drop on the floor!"

Lauren was about to leave so that Nella could nap when Nella said suddenly, "Have you heard anything from Eric?"

"No. He's busy and on the go with his research. Anyway, it's unlike him to write unless there's a crisis."

"But there is one, you know. His world has all but changed orbits."

"Eric! Something's happened to Eric?" Lauren's heart was in her throat. "Is he sick?"

"Heartsick might be the word," Nella said softly. "I'm hoping he will write to you. Until then, there's no way I can say more, baby."

A deep feeling of compassion swept over Lauren— the tender feelings she had managed to sublimate here temporarily. *Eric's heartsick, for whatever reason, and I'm—yes, I'm homesick...We should be together to comfort each other....*

Chapter Ten

The winter solstice was near. During the daytime
Lauren worked alongside Troy, aware that she clasped
her sketching pen with frenzied fingers. The children at
the mission kept their sober, dark eyes on the calendar,
checking it day by day as December 21 came closer.

"Will we finish in time?" Lauren asked worriedly,
flexing her fingers to increase the circulation.

Troy smiled. *"They* will," he assured her. "Are you
cold?" he asked suddenly.

"I'm all right," she said hastily. "It's just that the
boys and girl keep ahead of me with their carving.
They're better at whittling out the shepherds and wise
men than I am at drawing."

"Ah, but you are drawing *them*—drawing them to
you and, consequently, into learning the meaning of
the Holy Birth as I have never been able to explain
it before."

It was true, Lauren knew. A mutual love and trust

134

had taken root and grown to unbelievable proportions. The Eskimo children with their sparkling, almond-shaped eyes and the dark, pensive-eyed Indian boys and girls were her slaves. But what made her heart beat with joy was their grasp of the Christmas story, reflected first in the artistic characters carved in the totem pole for the potlash and then transferred into their English vocabularies.

" 'A little child shall lead them...' is certainly applicable here," Troy said appreciatively as Lauren was putting away the remains of the day's work one afternoon. "These children take home the message in a very meaningful way."

"I know," Lauren said, turning to meet his gaze briefly. "It has been a wonderful experience," she laughed, "one in which I have felt almost driven."

"I have sensed that in you. If I am not being too forward, may I ask whether this was because of inspiration—as I have hoped—or if it springs from another source?"

"Both," Lauren answered truthfully. "I *am* inspired. And that is why I felt a sense of urgency to see this through—before—"

Too late she realized that she was on the verge of disclosing more than she wished. Troy's dark eyes lit up with hope, and he moved quickly to take one of her hands gently in his own. Carefully the strong fingers massaged her own, as he had seen her do, gradually bringing back the flow of blood to the blanched tips.

Studying her hands, Troy whispered in the dark intimacy of the empty room, "May I believe that I have contributed to the happiness you have found here, my dear Lauren?"

"Oh, yes, Troy! You know you have—"

With his free hand Troy turned Lauren's face toward him, looking searchingly into her eyes. "Then dare I hope that there can be more between us—that you have come to realize that you do not love Tyrone Valdez and that the two of us—"

Lauren gently pulled her hand from this warm grasp and just as gently placed it against Troy's lips. His words were better unspoken.

"Please!" she implored softly with tears streaming down her cheeks. "Say no more. I am not free to love you—now or ever. You must believe that."

For one frightening moment Troy grasped the hand she had placed on his lips to silence the words that were painful for them both. Then, brushing each fingertip with a kiss, he let her hand drop from his.

Lauren wiped at her tears. In the blue half-light of fading day, she waited in the stillness for Troy's acceptance of her refusal, knowing that she had hurt this wonderful man.

But, when at last he spoke, it was to say, "Stay with me, Lauren...please stay..."

"I can't," she whispered, turning to the door of the darkening mission, wishing with all her heart that Troy Huguenot had been wrong in saying that we do not love others for their goodness...

The encounter left Lauren shaken and exhausted. At the same time it inspired her to take renewed interest in her book. What Troy said was true, she decided. It *had* to be true, because she said aloud with sudden realization, "God does not love us for our goodness either—but because of His."

She began to spend more and more of the long hours

of the evening studying the questionnaires on marriage. The findings might well prove to be more valuable to her, the writer, than to the readers. There were some answers, undefined as yet, that she hoped to find.

Visions of Eric's serious, achingly-familiar face, alongside Troy Huguenot's pained eyes at her rejection and Ty's compelling handsomeness floated between Lauren and the typed pages of the manuscript—but she doggedly read on. Surely, surely the pages would reveal some clue—something which would give substance to the ghosts of the past and the mysteries and fears of the present. *Maybe if I knew what went wrong between Mother and Daddy, I could understand*...Lauren realized then that this was the first time she had dared say her father's name, even to herself, since that fateful day when she and Eric had seen him holding another woman as he should have held his wife. "Daddy," she whispered, "Daddy!" The tears that came felt good. Something melted inside—something she did not understand, except that it was good...

Lauren thumbed through her survey with renewed interest. Skipping quickly through the statistics of age, current marital status, and details regarding education and church affiliations, she went to the heart of the research. When she reached the question she had posed, "Which of the following coincides most closely with your prayer practices?" Lauren paused. Prayer was *so* important, as were all of her questions regarding other religious practices and beliefs, and all of which she longed to be examining. But for now there was a sense of near-desperation in what the questionnaires might reveal on one area—one area alone.

"If you face a serious dilemma in your marital relationship or there has been a recent crisis, which do you believe?" With trembling fingers, Lauren smoothed out the pages posing the question and began a tabulation.

The hours went by unnoticed. When at last the figures were ready to total and figure into percentages, Lauren rested her cramped fingers and checked her watch. One A.M.! Where *had* the time gone?

No matter what the hour, she had to know the results. Most of the women (to her dismay) indicated that they were "being punished for their wrongdoings." Second in number were those who believed "I have sinned, and God will punish me in the hereafter." A large number of wives believed that "God will settle it in His own time." Lauren's eyes drifted to her final box beneath the question: *"The problem stems from the sins of my parents."*

"Only 4 percent!" she said aloud. Where could these women have been? How had they failed to know? Surely they had not read their Bibles!

Realizing then that the fire had died down and the once-warm front room had taken on a definite chill, Lauren quickly gathered her papers up and stacked them in preparation for leaving. Switching off the desk lamp, she was about to leave the room when there came a faint cry. At first she did not recognize the sound, but the second call was louder and more distinct—the unmistakable howl of a wolf. Instinctively she knew that it was the signal which had summoned Jessica two weeks ago.

Shivering with apprehension, she crept to the window and tried to see between the snowdrifts bordering the walk. It was harder to see from this point than it had been from her bedroom, and for a moment she saw no motion. Then slowly the faint outline of a man —it must be Ty—moved into the outer rim of light.

At the third, and louder, call, Lauren heard a movement in the outer hall. Easing into the shadow of a wing-backed chair, she waited breathlessly for Jessica to emerge from the front door as it opened with only a faint swish.

"Oh, no, it can't be!" The words of surprise were torn from her lips when she saw not one, but two, figures move down the path. Anna and Ivan Petrov!

Surely there was some mistake. With cold hands Lauren tried to clear away the steam from her own breath as she strained for a closer look. Even so, her vision was blurred by a sheet of ice which coated the window pane from the outside.

It would be easy to make a mistake. The ice gave a distorted view, much like a wavy mirror which pulls everything into ridiculous proportions. But if it wasn't the Petrovs, then *who?*

She strained harder to see, aware that the cold was seeping into her being and that her eyes were heavy-lidded from the long hours of reading. At that moment she made a decision—one totally unlike her, she knew, and one which the old Lauren of another time and place would never have ventured to make.

Without further thought, she pulled down the first warm parka she could find as she fumbled in the dark closet. The snow boots felt enormous, but they would have to do. No mittens. She would stuff her hands in the pockets. Noiselessly she eased open the front door and then the storm door. When they closed behind her, she crouched low and moved along the path.

At first there was not a sound. And then she heard the hum of voices on the still, bitterly cold night air. Even at a distance, one voice was easily distinguishable as that of Anna Petrov. The men's voices were muffled. She would have to move closer. Anna Petrov was speaking.

"The plane's ready for takeoff, you say? Loaded? But will the equipment be on hand for burying it before—"

At that moment Lauren felt a sudden spasm of her body and she sneezed. Any other time she could have stifled the sound. But, straining as she was to hear the words and still the chattering of her teeth, she had been unaware of the urge. There was an immediate silence, more frightening than sound. Danger...she must flee...

But it was too late. "Come out! This minute—unless you wish to be killed!"

Lauren could only suppose the low, harsh voice belonged to Ivan. Pressing her body against the snowbank, she weighed the possiblity of escape. *Ty! Where was Ty?* No matter how involved he was in this, he would see that no harm came to her.

With as much courage as she could muster, Lauren stepped around the bend of snow and into full view of a searchlight turned directly on her face with blinding force. Involuntarily she let out a little cry.

Rudely, the speaker seized both her arms and pulled her closer to the other two dark shadows.

"Well, what do you know? Our little missionary!"

There was a hiss of surprised breath from the other two, followed by Anna's mocking laugh on the brittle air. "Maybe she'd like to come along on a *real* mission. Well, what are you going to do, Ivan? Stand there until the other plane has left Nome while you decide what to do with a spy?"

"I'm no spy—I—I—" The cold sucked her breath away. The words froze in her throat.

"There is nothing to decide!" Ivan snapped. And, without further warning, he snatched the parka from Lauren's head, shoving something sharp and cold to her temple. A knife? Or was it a gun?

Feeling that she was taking part in an outdated, late-night movie, Lauren was only dimly aware of what happened next. Another hand seemed to be seizing the instrument, drawing it away from her head, and, blessedly, she heard Ty's voice!

"Let go of Lauren," he said in a flat voice.

"Are you out of your skull!" Anna, who had tried to move between the two men, spoke in an incredulous voice.

"Release her and put away the knife, Petrov. Unless you want your head blown off?"

"The others will get you. They'll get you both for this!" Ivan's growl said that he would see to it personally. But now he wavered.

"Perhaps," Ty said with a touch of authority. "But at the moment the gun is to my advantage."

Lauren felt Ivan's grip on her arm relax as Ty stepped closer. Then Ty spoke to her for the first time: "Get back to the inn, you little fool—and nobody is to know. Do you understand?"

Hardly feeling the rude shake Ty gave her, Lauren stumbled blindly back toward the inn. But, overcome by exhaustion, shock, and cold, she collapsed just outside the door.

Somebody was dragging her inside. It didn't matter who. Nothing mattered. Her body seemed to be on fire with numbness that extended to her heart, leaving only her brain clear to think. Ty was involved in something illegal. Ty had betrayed her. He had misused her and her friends. Was there nobody—*nobody* she could trust?

"I keep trying...*(why was she so sleepy?)*... to make everybody happy...*(and her tongue so thick?*... but it's never enough...I ought to do better...*be* better..."

"To yourself, yes!" Jessica spoke sharply. *Jessica?* With quick, impatient hands, the other girl was stripping off Lauren's clothes with such furious yanks that surely there must be a layer of skin coming off in the process. At first Lauren hardly felt the roughness of the rubdown that followed. Then, slowly—as the strong, efficient hands massaged her body—a faint tingle set in.

"You've got to have a stimulant. There's brandy—"

"No!" Lauren sat bolt upright. "I don't use strong drink! A rule—"

She sank back onto the couch where Jessica had half-lifted her a few moments earlier, wondering why the sudden nausea. She closed her eyes and listened weakly as Jessica mumbled something indistinguishable about "puritanism" and stirred the contents of a glass vigorously.

"Drink this!"

"What—"

"Hot tea in lieu of cooperation! Better for you than coffee." Jessica inhaled deeply. "How long have you known you had Raynaud's disease?"

"Just since I came here. But—but—" She sank back

exhausted. How ridiculous to be discussing her health when there was a crisis going on outside, just yards away from the window above their heads. Ty might, at this very moment, be dying! "Jessica, there's trouble. I—he—"

Almost rudely, Lauren felt herself pushed back down onto the couch. "Say nothing more!" Jessica commanded sharply. "The less you know, the safer—and, whatever you do, trust nobody. Nobody including me. *Especially* me!"

When Lauren was a little stronger, Jessica insisted that they get back to their rooms. Undetected, they made it down the hall, and with the other girl's help Lauren was able to get between the blankets. She closed her eyes in relief. But it was only for a moment. There was a soft tap-tap on the door followed by a hollow whisper.

"Let me in, Lauren—quickly!"

Ty! Lauren knew a moment's relief. Then she clutched at the covers in fear. She was to trust no one, Jessica had warned. And Jessica didn't know half of it!

"Open it! Do you want me killed?"

Ty's whisper was hoarse. Remembering the nightmarish scene in the snow, Lauren struggled into her robe and slippers and unbolted the door.

"You ought not be here," she whispered. "The others—what will they think—and—oh, Ty, you're injured!"

Lauren saw a quick stab of light from beneath Jessica's door. "Get inside—hurry!" she whispered and bolted the door. "Now—let me look at you."

In the dimness of the outside light she was able to see a jagged gash cut in his parka. Around it was a

ring of fresh blood. Surely the wound must be dangerously near the heart. Quickly she drew the heavy drapes
closed and turned on the small lamplight. As best she
could, Lauren cleaned and disinfected the wound,
noting gratefully that the bleeding had stopped.

"We have to get help, Ty," Lauren said when she
had done the best she could with her few first-aid
supplies.

There was no answer. She saw then that he had
fallen into a deep sleep born of exhaustion and loss
of blood.

"What can I do, Lord? He can't stay here. But he's
not able to move—and, anyway, if I tell the others—
oh, dear God, *speak* to me! *What can I do?*"

A few minutes later, Lauren knew what she must
do. Her responsibility was laid out as clearly as if the
Lord had said quietly, "You know what you must do,
child. Minister to the sick."

No matter what this man had done, *she* had done
the right thing. In the morning she would have to set
everything straight. But right now she would have to
leave things as they were. Lives might depend upon
it—his, hers, everybody's at the inn. So thinking,
Lauren pulled extra blankets from the chest and
covered Ty's still, limp form where he lay on the foot
of the bed. Too exhausted to think further, she crawled
as far to the head of the bed as possible, pulled the
heavy blankets tightly beneath her chin, and decided
to keep watch until the rest of the dreadful night was
past. But her eyelids drooped. And sleep came.

It was there that Nella found them when there was
no answer to her repeated knocks at the door the
following morning...

Chapter Eleven

During the three days that followed, Ty hovered between life and death. "I've lived through worse, my dear, let me assure you—and this is no exception," he repeated feverishly over and over.

Dr. Piriot, however, was less certain. "If only he had come to me at once," he said regretfully, "perhaps we could have avoided the blood poisoning. The loss of blood is against him, too."

Lauren, burdened by guilt at her own negligence, stayed by Ty's bed around the clock. No amount of coaxing could bring her from his side. Except for her, he wouldn't have the wound in the first place, she reasoned. He had tried to protect her. And, except for her fear of being found out, she would have summoned the doctor against his wishes that night. That made her responsible on two counts—maybe three—because deep inside there was a nagging feeling that, in spite of all that Ty was involved in, she had helped bring him here.

During the lonely hours of vigil, while Lauren allowed Jessica and Dr. Piriot to sleep briefly, she found herself in frequent dialogue with herself. It was as if the "two Laurens" spoke in conflict.

What do you expect of all this? one part of her asked the other.

Why—that Ty will have some explantions, the other part would reason.

You know better!

It was true. The suspicion, which had begun with Ty's arrival—no, farther back, when he had her mail the letter, or even from the moment of his impetuous proposal—enlarged like a summer storm cloud. Ultimately it could destroy!

But, no, she must not think such things. Ty had saved her life. Ty loved her. And, so, the other Lauren insisted, *he wants to marry me.*

Does he love you?

Now that's Aunt Nella thinking, the defensive Lauren would say. *Of course he loves me! We'll work at it—*

Aha! The first Lauren would scoff. *So the "work ethic" creeps in!*

Now that's Troy thinking. And he's out of my life. I don't love him.

But the other Lauren would not let her square the corners of her past and fold them away. *Ah, Lauren, Lauren, are you so blind that your heart can no longer guide you? You're searching for what you left behind. Only you are too guilt-ridden to acknowledge it!*

After one such conversation with herself, Lauren in desperation dropped to her knees beside Ty's bed.

It was imperative that he live.

"Lord, I beg You to save him. Preserve Ty's life—and whatever he's involved in, rescue him from that too. He needs Your presence here, Lord. Mine isn't enough." Then, realizing that she was resorting to her guilt even in talking with Him who knew her heart better than she knew it herself, Lauren amended her prayer: "Forgive me for putting down myself, Your daughter, redeemed by Your love—for not recognizing that I *am* needed here, for not believing in Your power to heal. Together we have a big job to do, Lord. And I'll stick by!"

As Lauren sobbed into her clenched fists, she was unaware that a quiet figure had entered the room and knelt down beside her. And then she heard the deep intonations of one of Troy's prayers that he said during the services at the mission. When the prayer was finished, she murmured an *"Amen"* with him and stood, realizing that a strange peace had come. Tears of gratitude welled up and spilled down her cheeks.

Troy looked into her eyes. "Oh, Lauren," he said brokenly. "It is a miracle that you could pray for the man with more grace than I am able to manage. Surely your prayers will be heard above those I am able to send up this day. You see, it is my calling to care about the spirit of mankind—but his demise means—it means nothing to me at all. It is for me that you must pray."

Ty stirred ever so slightly, and Troy Huguenot left as silently as he had entered...

Dr. Piriot came in then and took over with the sick man. And in the morning, after Lauren had napped briefly in a chair in the corner of Ty's room, the doctor said that Ty would live. He also said that

Ty wanted to talk to Lauren—alone.

Ty lay wan and spent against the whiteness of the pillow, but there was a flicker of the old fire in his dark eyes. And for once Lauren welcomed the faintly-mocking smile.

"I told you I would survive," he said.

"And I praise the Lord for your recovery."

Ty shrugged. "As you will," he said. "Tell me, my dear, why did you not tell all the others? Why did you protect me?"

"Don't think I wasn't tempted!" Lauren answered.

As usual, she had amused him, but it was good to see his smile broaden. "Maybe you should have, you know—that way you wouldn't have been forced to marry me."

"Whatever are you talking about?"

"Well," Ty paused, obviously enjoying himself, "we *did* spend the night together, you know. You even saw to it that there were witnesses."

Lauren felt her face grow hot. "If you think for one minute—"

"It's not what I think. It's what *they* think."

But before she could respond to the ludicrous words, Ty—his mood having changed with his usual suddenness—grasped Lauren's wrists and, with surprising strength, pulled her toward him.

"Sit here beside me—not there—here on the bed. Come, come, don't be coy. We've shared a bed before, remember!"

Speechless, Lauren sat down gingerly on the edge of the bed. To her relief, Ty let go of her wrists.

"The doctor has told me to keep this brief, so I'll come right to the point. How much did you overhear?"

Lauren told him, ending with, "And no matter what you are about to tell me, Ty, I do want to thank you for saving my life."

"As I thank you for saving my skin. But there is something more I must ask of you, Lauren."

"I refuse to be involved in this scam—whatever it is. And, Ty, you've told me nothing."

"There was no opportunity until now. And even now the time's limited until Dr. Piriot and Jessica check on us. So, listen, will you, without interrupting? You *are* involved. We all are!"

Fear clutched at her heart. But, wordlessly, she nodded.

"There will be people here soon—anytime now—investigating two matters. One I wish you to be informed about. The other," he paused, "I do not want you involved in. You see, you are a witness to both in a sense—one which will help apprehend and hopefully break up a spy ring—"

"*Spy!*" Involuntarily the whisper came from Lauren's dry lips.

Ty ignored the interruption. "And the other—well, the other has to do with me and my business here. I may be investigated too. But, Lauren," Ty moved restlessly against his pillow, and Lauren saw that his strength was failing. He moistened his lips. "Lauren, it isn't as bad as you have chosen to believe. Against your codes and creeds, I am sure, but, my dear, so many things are! As to being illegal, however, no. So I must ask you to help protect me. Have I a promise?"

Lauren shook her head sadly. "No, Ty," she said softly, "except on the condition that I know from what and from whom I am protecting you."

Ty appeared to weigh the alternatives. Then, slowly, he spoke. "I don't know what's come over me, unless it's you and this God of yours," he said as if he disbelieved his own behavior, "but I am gullible enough to trust you."

"You really have little choice." Lauren said tartly.

"Government agents will undoubtedly be here to pick up the Petrov pair. They're not newlyweds, you know. They're brother and sister, a team from Russia, here to gather secret information—hopefully from the load I supervised having brought here—"

"Of what?" Lauren asked desperately.

"Ah, my dear, here is where we reach a parting of the ways—atomic waste. But, before you run screaming for the F.B.I., just rest assured that the government knows what my mission is—"

"Do you mean," Lauren began slowly, for it was becoming more clear in her mind what Ty must be doing here in this remote section of Alaska, "that you are supervising the unloading and burying of waste *here?* With the government's approval?"

"With government *orders*," he corrected.

"You mean you would do that with no regard for human life or danger to wildlife here, not knowing the outcome—how *could* you?" Lauren drew back in shock such as she had not known since the Day of Discovery for herself and Eric.

"Don't you think we've experimented enough to know that, as far as we can determine, we are doing none of those things? Don't you know that our government would never *knowingly* destroy its people or the flora and fauna of the land?"

"Knowingly," she mocked. "You see, they don't

know what will happen generations from now."

"And you do?"

"I know," Lauren said slowly. "I know that the sins of the fathers are visited upon their children. The Bible is my authority."

"I can't argue that one, being no scholar. But, then, neither am I bound by it—I can't even pretend to understand what it means. You know," the old Tyrone Valdez paused with a twinkle in his eyes, "if we were at leisure, I would press you to interpret that verse."

When Lauren started to protest, Ty raised a hand to silence her. "We do not have the leisure! As I told you, everything is above-board. Some day you and the rest of the world will understand that we've taken every precaution."

"And until then, the devil take the hindmost!" Lauren burst out angrily. "You don't care what happens to these people! You called them tourists. You—you—take pleasure in this!"

"Whoa, whoa! I did not choose the spot. But, yes, I confess that I find a certain excitement in my job. There are those who don't agree, of course, and that is where I need your help, my dear Lauren. We can expect the environmentalists to come tapping on the door at any moment. Please keep my whereabouts to yourself. I wish to answer to my immediate superior, not the fish and game commission or the state's natural resources board!"

Lauren sat silent, her hands clasped so tightly that the knuckles stood out white against the black checks of her woolen pants. Staring straight ahead, she said in a pained voice, "You never loved me at all, did you, Ty?"

"You would not believe me if I said I did."

"You never said it."

Ty's voice was tired. "All right, then. I didn't. Not until now. I was charmed by your—" He paused as if seeking a word.

"Strangeness," she supplied.

"I was going to say *difference*, but I believe I like *strangeness* better—charmingly so. Then, I needed a contact—"

"And so you made use of this 'strange person.' "

Ty winced and Lauren knew that she had hurt him. "If it's any consolation, my dear, I fell in love with you—as much as I am capable of loving—but I can see now that I have spoiled whatever chances I might have had, have I not?"

At her nod, he continued, "I understand. So, if you will do this one thing for me, I will get out of your life—once and for all. Just bid me good riddance and forget this chapter."

"You know that will not happen," she said truthfully, "but, yes, I will help you —although, for the life of me, I don't know why."

As Lauren turned toward the door with tears in her eyes, she heard him say humbly, "I know why, Lauren. It is because you are a fine person. Would it make you happy if I gave some thought to this God of yours? Think He could patch up my life for me, do you?"

"I know He can," she said and turned away before Ty could see the tears that washed down her cheeks. Broken love affairs were not easy. She had gone through too many of late. Ty had hurt her...she had hurt Troy...and she and Eric had hurt each other...

But, even as Lauren closed the door softly behind her, she felt an upward swing of her heart. There were a million questions that needed answering. But, basically, the episode was finished. There was no pain—just a sort of sadness.

She hurried down the halls toward her wing of the inn. "I'll take a long bath and sleep for a week," she murmured aloud as she entered her own room.

Happier than she had been for a long time, Lauren poured a generous amount of lilac bubble bath into the tub and turned the hot water on full-blast. Humming a little tune, she sorted through her dinner clothes and decided on the fuschia velvet that she had worn the night of Ty's arrival. As she laid it across the foot of the bed and opened the drawer of her dressing table to get her pearls, a packet of letters fell from on top of her hairbrush, where somebody had propped them. Airmail—all of them—she saw at a quick glance.

Quickly she picked them up. Eric's name appeared in the upper lefthand corner of each envelope! The return addresses each different from the other—strange, exotic-sounding cities in Old Mexico. With a pounding heart, Lauren ran barefoot to the tub, turned the water off, and snuggled beneath the covers for warmth as, with trembling fingers she opened the first of the stack. But, even before she read, Lauren's mind raced ahead to wonder where the letters could have been delayed—unless, she thought suddenly, they were apprehended like the oranges. Obviously they had not been tampered with...and where they had been was of no great consequence at the moment. Eric had written. *Oh, praise the Lord, she and Eric were in touch!*

Chapter Twelve

Paying no attention to dates, Lauren began reading the letter on the top of the stack. Eric was in the vanilla jungle, he wrote, and went on to describe it so vividly that Lauren could smell the blossoms, hear the calls of the birds he told about, and feel the warm winds caress her face. In fantasy, she walked by his side, drinking in nature the way the two of them had always done. With a faint smile, she laid the first letter aside, wondering dreamily if vanilla blossoms had long stems like the "evening glories" from which she and Eric could sip honey from the ends...

The second letter included a brief report of his success with the California State Committee on Wildlife Preservation. Eric had experienced "measureable success with that august body," he wrote. They had agreed to take his suggestions regarding preservation of the Torrey Pines under advisement. A thrill of excitement began in the region of her heart and raced to her fingertips when he ended with, "I will want your help on submitting plans for the one area we designated as our 'marriage temple'... remember?"

Hungrily Lauren scanned the next letter, savoring every word, as she read of Eric's research in oceanography. He had begun his dissertation—the hardest part, he said. How well she knew!

Lauren laid the letter aside momentarily and gave in to the urge to live in the past again—just briefly. She and Eric, orphaned urchins of the sea, walked barefoot on the beaches. What was it that Eric had said? Slowly the words came back: "How many tracks will be washed away, filled up with sand, rubbed out by the tracks of others? Will any of them leave a path?"

Even as a child, Eric had spoken no idle words— riddles, sometimes, but never idle. Always the words had more than one meaning...like the shifting sands of time...and their responsibility to leave "a something" for those who came after us. That was one's purpose on this earth, Eric said. "We must learn to smell a million flowers and not touch one. God gave us dominion over the flowers and trees, the sea and all within it!"

"And God gave you dominion over my heart, Eric!" The words were wrenched from Lauren before she knew they were coming. Then she sat quietly for a long, long time. "The words are out, Lord," she whispered at last. "And words can never be unsaid. I love Eric with all my being, Lord. You know I do. I know it is wrong...but what can I do?"

If she could cry, she would feel better. But she was dry-eyed. What was it that tugged away at her mind? Something he had said in one of his several references to *generations*.

Then suddenly she knew. How odd that Ty himself would have entered into the picture! In the heaviness of their conversation less than an hour earlier, Ty had challenged her interpretation of the Scripture—the one under which she and Eric had lived for so many years.

Quickly Lauren picked up her Bible and with trembling fingers turned to the fatal passage. Even when she located the verse, it took courage to look. She had never dared reread it since that awful day, and even now there came the childish feeling that she might be struck dead if she so much as looked upon the words in search of new meaning. *Whatever happens,* she promised herself, *I will fit myself into God's pattern—not try to fit Him into mine.* And with that thought she read Deuteronomy 5:9. Once, twice, then three times she read it. Then, laying the Bible aside—still open at the account of Moses' delivery of the Commandments—Lauren lay staring at the ceiling.

How could she—how could *they*—have taken a section of one verse out of context and fashioned it into a yoke? As children that was understandable. She and Eric, crumpled and small, forlorn and abandoned, had crept into The Little Church of the Sands in seek of a refuge. In search of love, too, which their parents had taken from them. They had found the love, or at least its beginning—as much as they could comprehend. *Somebody* loved them. Even now Lauren was grateful to that quiet man in the long black robe who introduced them to God. Neither the Eldridges nor the Thornes had bothered...

But as adults why hadn't one or both of them gone back before now and reread the verse in its entirety? Closing her eyes, Lauren repeated the passage aloud:

"Thou shalt not bow down thyself unto them [graven images], nor serve them; for I the Lord thy God am a jealous God, visiting the iniquity of the fathers upon the children unto the third and fourth generation of them that hate me."

A smile which began in Lauren's heart slowly touched her lips, curving them into a gentle smile. "Why, I don't hate You, Lord—I *love* you! And I can never, ever bow down to other gods. In fact, Lord," she hesitated, realizing then that the words she was about to say were new to her but something the Lord had known all along, "I will never be the fulfilled person I long to be until I find a way to serve You...I can never be satisfied until I go into Christian work of some sort...I want to be Your servant..."

The smile broadened, and suddenly Lauren felt herself laughing with something which she could describe better as *joy* than *happiness*. She wasn't accountable for the sins of her parents. God held her accountable only for her *own* actions. "Oh, Lord," she said in a loud, clear voice, "I can't wait till I tell Eric!"

As much as she loved the velvet dress, Lauren hung it back in the closet, choosing instead her long black skirt and a ruffled, demurely high-necked blouse. She loved the feminine style of the blouse, but the absence of color determined tonight's choice. The white seemed perfect for her deep sense of peace. Nobody else would know that, purged of her guilt, Lauren felt as pure of heart as the blouse was free of color...refreshed...cleansed...wonderful!

★   ★   ★

The sense of peace lingered—a blessing in the busy

days that followed. Because of it, the swift-moving, dramatic, and unexpected events somehow seemed less traumatic. Lauren had only one regret: Business kept her so occupied that she was unable to get back to her personal life. Many pieces of the puzzle here at the inn remained to be put together. Her book waited for additional work. Even Eric's precious letters went unread. Because of the heavy demands on her time, Lauren was unable to find even stolen moments of solitude. She coveted those moments—especially to read the letters. But by the time she was able to get back to them, she found that Eric and his letters themselves were a vital part of the puzzle.

Only three days remained until the villagers would turn their calendars to December 21. It was the winter solstice—the date set for the potlash, and the great day when new totem poles would go up in Kakalota, especially the ones depicting the Christmas story on which they had worked so feverishly.

Lauren checked on Ty's progress but purposely avoided his company. They had said their good-byes. She would stick by her commitment to him, and she expected that he would make good his promise to her and be out of her life as soon as Dr. Piriot pronounced him well enough.

There would have been no time for visiting even had circumstances been different. "I so hesitate to ask this of you, Lauren, but is it possible that we could spend some evenings working on details for the celebration? We are running behind—" Troy had said uncertainly.

"Of course," she had answered. And together they had worked 12 hours that day.

It was almost midnight when Troy bade her good

night and went to his room. Lauren picked up her working materials and turned off the light in the front room in preparation for returning to her wing.

At that moment there was a light rap on the outside door, followed by the chime of sleighbells which told her that the caller had located the latch thong. That meant a stranger!

Lauren hesitated. Should she call Troy back? No, by now he would have crossed several of the icy halls. Turning the light back on, she went to the door, intending to open it only a crack and inquire who was there. But the wind cut through the opening with razor-sharpness, pushing the door from her hands. There was no recourse but to invite the person or persons inside and hurry back through the first door.

There were two men, each of them bundled in parkas. She wondered why they had come, and how.

The taller of the two men spoke first: "Sorry for the instrusion, miss. My name is Yorkshire—Federal Bureau of Investigation."

Lauren felt her hand go to her heart involuntarily. Seeing the gesture, the man said reassuringly, "There is no need for alarm, Miss—"

"Eldridge," she supplied. "Lauren Eldridge."

The other man stepped forward. "You are the one we wished to see. I am Burton Quine, also of the F.B.I. We understand from Tyrone Valdez that you are willing to identify two guests here, Ivan and Anna Petrov?"

Mutely she nodded.

"And perhaps to give us additional information as to what happened on the night of December 14?"

Realizing that the men were cold and still standing, Lauren invited them to be seated and checked to see if coffee remained in the pot. Finding it still hot, she poured two cups with as much poise as she could manage while they peeled off the fur-lined parkas.

Their faces were as reassuring as their badges—brisk and businesslike but courteous. And their questions were easy to answer. She dreaded the indentification. But, to her immense relief, Burton Quine said, "You have been a great help, Miss Eldridge. If you can identify these pictures?"

There was no mistaking the photographs. When she nodded, the man who introduced himself as Yorkshire said, "Now, if you could direct us—"

"I will take over from here!" A voice said from the door. And there, to her amazement, stood Ty, white and shaken, but very much at ease. Greeting the men by name, he shook their hands. Then, with a little mock salute, he dismissed Lauren.

There were no more than two hours left before the breakfast call, Lauren realized, as she undressed quickly and crawled into the woolly comfort of her blanket-spread bed. Even so, Ty's face kept floating between her and the world of sleep. It was strange— her feeling for the man. Strange in that it was love— not the kind that is akin to the infatuation she had felt upon first meeting him and certainly not the kind upon which one builds a marriage, but a love that was deeper, more compassionate and understanding.

The winds, having iced the world anew, subsided. Lauren turned the calendar in the mission to December 19. Two days remaining. The children were so excited that their little square-fingered hands shook as they shaved, carved, and polished each intricate figuring. Over and over, as they worked, they begged for the

Christmas story. And, tirelessly, Lauren repeated it to
the mission chidren—and to their parents, for now that
the excitement had reached its peak, the men and
women of the village had gathered to help. In their
eyes, Lauren saw the same look of bewilderment
followed by a certain degree of understanding—and,
finally, a look of sheer joy.

"If only you could stay, my dear Lauren," Troy
ventured in a low tone at one point. "Don't you see
what we could do together?"

"Don't, Troy," she said softly. "It's quite
impossible."

"But where will you go? What will you do—after
this?" He spread his hands wide to indicate the bless-
ings they both felt.

"I don't know," she answered slowly. "Wherever the Lord sends me—but somewhere into some
kind of Christian service."

The gentle man nodded with understanding, then
shook his head sadly. Lauren turned away from his
pained face. The might-have-been expression on the
sensitive features wrenched at her heart...

Shortly after dinner that evening, she and Troy
began to put the final touches to the drawings for the
children. But the newsletter remained. Together they
had composed an odd but intelligible Christmas story
by means of French and simple English, punctuated
with frequent pictures repeated over and over for
clarity. Troy had drafted a touching holiday message
and Lauren did a lot of fantasy pictures of Christmas
trees, bells, candy canes, and a sleighful of toys pulled
by reindeer. They would be finished this evening, Troy
said, looking over her shoulder with pleasure.

And perhaps they would have, except for Dr. Piriot's sobering news. "There is something going around in the village—not contagious, apparently, but more puzzling because it isn't, I guess."

"What are the symptoms, Doctor?" Troy asked with concern.

But even before the answer came, Lauren knew what it would be. The words, when spoken, caused her heart to flutter and then seem to stop.

"Nausea, headache, general malaise—Lauren! Are you all right?"

All right? No! Of course I am not all right. Not when the children I love may have been exposed to radiation! But maybe she was wrong. Ty had told her precautions had been taken...and she had promised, *Dear Lord, take care of it! And help me stand by.*

"I'm fine," Lauren answered firmly. "Now, if you will help me with the message you wish to send our people—" So together the three of them worked on. Twelve o'clock. One. Two!

Wearily Lauren prepared for bed. She was about to turn out the bedlight when she heard the shuffle of footsteps near her door. Who? And what? At this hour? The Petrovs were gone. Ty was in the clear. Then who was the intruder?

Before she could think of what to do, however, there was a soft *tap-tap* on her door. "May I come in? Please, Lauren."

The words were a near-whisper, but Lauren recognized the voice as Jessica's. What could she want at this unearthly hour? And what could the two of them possibly have to say to each other?

"Please, Lauren—I'm freezing!"

Quickly Lauren unbolted the door. "Come inside," she said briskly.

Once inside, Jessica flexed her fingers to warm them, then folded her hands together, bringing the sleeves of her fleecy robe together like a muff. *How lovely she is,* Lauren thought, quickly noting the dark hair framing the ivory face in which the blue, blue eyes glistened like the blue-white shadows of the frozen North. *Ice Princess. That describes Jessica Piriot.*

"Let's get right down to business," Jessica said abruptly. Then, seating herself on the edge of the bed, she motioned for Lauren to sit beside her as if she—not Lauren—were the hostess.

"There's a lot that needs explaining, and the fewer questions you ask until I'm finished, the better. Agreed?" At Lauren's nod, she added. "Even then, there are a good many I'll be unable to answer."

"Unable or unwilling?" Lauren asked softly.

"Both." And with that word, Jessica told Lauren an incredible story in a flat, emotionless voice that sounded as if the two of them were totally uninvolved instead of the two central figures.

She, Jessica, was all she appeared to be—a trained nurse and the niece of Andre Piriot. Those things and "more." How much more was one of the matters which must go unexplained forever. Otherwise, she would be unable to fulfill her other missions here. Did Lauren understand? When on "special assignment," it was necessary to employ whatever means necessary to see it through. Example: apprehension and arrest of the Petrovs...nothing personal, you know, just a job which required careful screening of everything and everybody until it was determined if there was a "conspiracy'' or a "ring''—and, speaking of rings, yes, the gold signet rings that she and Ty wore were identifications. They had never met and—

"Then Ty is also a—whatever it is that you are— besides the job of—his other job?" The words rushed out quickly as Lauren felt that she had to know the answer. But in her eagerness she realized too late that she may have been on the verge of revealing more than she should. How much did Jessica know? she wondered.

"Yes, he was on assignment here—as well as being here on other business." Jessica's shrug indicated that she neither knew nor cared about Ty's other work.

Neither Jessica nor Ty had met Anna and Ivan Petrov (not their real names) but knew them by photograph. Jessica "played it cool," she said, until Ty could make contact with Anna. The letter Lauren mailed? The same. There had been a bad moment when Anna stole the signet ring—yes, stole it—from Jessica's room. Fortunately, in her haste, the secret agent dropped the identifying piece of jewelry. And, even more fortunately, it was Lauren who found it.

"Well," Jessica inhaled deeply, and for the first time Lauren noted the violet rings of fatigue around the other girl's eyes. "That about sums it up, I guess— except for the real reason I came. I realize my timing was terrible—"

"It's all right, Jessica. But, yes, I wonder why you came."

"To explain what I could, and to apologize. I've been rude—purposely rude. I've invaded your privacy. I—I even made a play for your fiancee'. You *are* going to be married now that this is cleared up?"

Lauren shook her head. When Jessica's eyes narrowed slightly, Lauren went on to say, "Which has nothing to do with Troy, if that's what you're thinking. It's all very complicated—very hard to explain. But there's another man in my life," she blurted suddenly, wondering at the same time how the two of them, so alienated by circumstance, could be exchanging confidences like sorority sisters.

"Eric?"

"Eric," Lauren said sadly. "But don't ask me to explain—that relationship is quite out of the question too."

"Don't let it be, Lauren! Don't let anything stand in your way!" Jessica's voice was low and passionate. The ice in her blue eyes turned to flame. "Nothing can stop me from winning Troy. *Nothing!*"

Jessica paused for breath and then grinned wickedly. "We're more alike than he cares to acknowledge, you know—solid, stoic, *Alaskan,* which means cautious but hard-loving. We'll *work* it out in spite of 'His Holiness's' objection to the phrase!"

Both girls laughed, then fell into self-conscious silence. Jessica rose abruptly. "I hope we can be friends, as you suggested when you first came, Lauren. After all, we are going to be cousins, you know."

"You mean—" Lauren was too startled to finish the question.

Jessica nodded. "I mean!" She laughed. "My Uncle Andy is marrying your Aunt Nella. They've kept it so secret, I'm surprised that *they* found out!"

Stunned to silence, Lauren watched Jessica cross the room. But at the door the other girl paused. "About this Eric—I'm sorry about the oranges. All I wanted was his address in case—it's all a part of my job. And the letters—I had Tuk bring them in so I wouldn't be 'breaking and entering.' You did find them and read—"

"I haven't finished," Lauren answered. "There's been no time—you'd have to read his letters, and listen to him, to understand—"

"I understand enough to see that you're in love. Hopelessly. Head over heels. I applaud you. And, Lauren, I hope that my having to contact him made no difference. I had to tell him, you know—hoping to delay his possibly coming here—"

Jessica had been in touch with Eric? Suddenly Lauren's fatigue was gone. Her entire being was awake, alert, energized.

"What did you tell him Jessica? Oh, what have you done?"

"Why, that you and Tyrone Valdez were engaged. You'll find it in his letters. It's something the two of you can straighten out."

And, having shattered Lauren's life completely, Jessica was gone...

Chapter Thirteen

The call to breakfast brought Lauren back from a nether world of sleep into which she had fallen reluctantly after Jessica left. With all her heart she had wanted to read Eric's letters. No longer could she wait in order to savor each word and to dream impossible dreams. It was imperative now that the messages be read in an orderly fashion...the envelopes stacked chronologically, the corners squared...Jessica had told Eric...*what*...but sleep had intervened.

"I'm exhaused—totally and completely," Lauren told her pale reflection in the mirror. She paused just before touching her lips with gloss. *How,* she wondered, staring at her leaden-eyed self, *does a nervous breakdown commence?* Aloud, she said, "I am not sure I can face this day."

Did she imagine it or did the other Lauren, the one in the mirrror, move her lips? *Feeling guilty, aren't you? In spite of all your good intentions! You know you should have told Eric about Ty.*

Yes, I should have, Lauren admitted to her reflection. *But,* squaring her shoulders, *I am not going to feel guilty because—*

The two Laurens stared at each other. Then nodding in agreement as Lauren murmured and her reflection silently mouthed: "I am not going to wear a yoke of guilt again—not ever again. I will find a way to explain —I *will* find a way—because the Lord is my strength!"

The Lauren who greeted the other diners looked vibrant and fit. Nobody would have guessed that she had had one hour of dark sleep, that she was exhausted to the point of falling ill, and that inside, chafing and paining, was a rock where her heart should have been. Serenely she dined, taking coffee to revive her in spite of Dr. Piriot's warning glance. And serenely she turned the calendar at the mission school. December 20!

In spite of the children's excitement and the gathering of the adults for decorating the mission, Lauren and Troy were able to bring the day to a close early. The last festoon was hung. The last gift lay, shimmering and mysterious, beneath the tree that the two of them had fashioned with poles and crepe paper. The sky looked even darker than usual, even in the dim half-light typical of the winter solstice. Another storm?

But Troy's concern lay with the health of the children. Several more had fallen prey to the strange illness. "It's puzzling" he frowned. "Dr. Piriot's having the water tested and some soil examined."

"For what?" she asked with a catch in her voice.

"Some kind of contamination." With that, he locked the door and they descended the mountain to the inn, Troy scanning the sky as he drove.

Dark clouds formed themselves into towering banks,

and there was an air of eerie stillness between blasts of Arctic air. As Troy helped Lauren from the snowmobile, she felt herself being wrenched from his hand by a powerful gust of wind. Helplessly she stumbled and fell.

Nella met them at the door, swinging it open as another powerful gust struck the inn with such fury that the wooden frame shook. Closing the door against the storm once they were all inside, Nella said, "Let me have a look at the two of you. Anyway, I want to talk with you, Lauren."

"And *I* with *you*," Lauren replied. The slight emphasis on the words brought a blush to her aunt's face. "But for now I need to change clothes and," she looked out the window uneasily, "check on possible arrangements for tomorrow."

"We'll need to think of a fitting send-off for Ty, Lauren," Nella called after her retreating figure. "He will be strong enough to leave soon, Dr. Piriot says."

"Is *that* what my Uncle Andy says?" Lauren teased over her shoulder.

In her room, Lauren did not work on the arrangements she had mentioned. The potlash was under control, if the weather would cooperate. Without taking time to change, she reached for Eric's letters and, resisting the temptation to tear hungrily into the one on top, she stacked them according to the date of the postmark.

The first one told Lauren of oranges Eric was sending, and little else except to ask if she remembered where they left off their last game. Lauren laid the letter aside with a sad smile.

The second and third letters she had already read,

so she hurriedly opened the fourth in Eric's series of six. Quickly she scanned the brief page. Eric was continuing his research...the writing was going well...mail delivery was slow in Mexico...would she like to surprise him with a reply at his next address? Lauren wondered vaguely at the address and laid the letter with the others she had read. Except for the first note, Eric had made no mention of their childhood game—probably because he was getting no response. Oh, there would be so much to explain.

Almost frenzied by the thought, Lauren picked up the next letter. Only one more remained after this.

"Knock-knock...'First!' " it began, to Lauren's surprise. Quickly she read the first line: "Before proceeding, go back three steps. Pick up the questionnaire your mother mailed and read the attached. Then stop and think before proceeding with this letter."

Where *were* the questionnaires? Lauren tore through the stack. When finally she found it, she felt strangely as if her life depended upon the message. It was so like Eric. Yet it was so *unlike* Eric. It was both Erics—the strange child and the strange adult—with something new added. It was an Eric she did not understand, because it was too good to be true.

> My Dear Lauren:
>   I have been looking at some real estate—worthless by worldly values, but high on a mountian peak, closed in by stars. It's an odd kind of mountain, with pines and guaranteeing privacy. If we cleared a spot at the very top, we could build a house on a spaceship plan, glassed

in for a view in all directions. No garden
to hoe, but maybe a hive of bees for
sustenance? We can write to our hearts'
content, then read each other's writing. We
can go for long walks down our private
mountain, then back up again, wearing
hobnail boots—weighted, of course,
because the air is light in the 10-mile eleva-
tion. Let the years slip by—40, 50, who's
counting? After a hundred or so, perhaps
we'll lie down for the Long Slumber, miles
closer to heaven on our mountaintop, and
there God will find us. Because only He
will know.

—Amen.

Half-jesting, half-serious, and not smiling. Lauren
could see Eric through her tears as he wrote the letter.
It was clear that he felt as she did...but her elation died
with the thought that nothing had changed...had it?
Almost fearfully, she clutched the letter and resumed
reading the three lines.

She read, but she did not understand. What could
it mean? Whatever could it mean? "We are not
brother and sister—not even related. Why don't you
have your aunt explain as my father has explained to
me? He and Aunt Berta see each other. Both well. *All's*
well. 'Last...' Eric."

In her elation, Lauren was not sure whether to let
out a whoop that would shake Alaska loose from the
map, sob until she was devoid of tears, or kneel in a
prayer that went on for hours.

She must talk to Nella—and there remained one

letter in the stack from Eric. There wasn't time for both, and the choice she made was no choice at all. The letter, of course!

Reading did not take long once the envelope was open. There were three paragraphs—three short paragraphs that tore her world apart like the fantasy it was—the sharp, ugly, kaleidoscopic shards shattering at her feet.

Paragraph 1: Eric, still concerned with conservation, was accepting a government appointment to check on "atmospheric disturbances" to wildlife while continueing his treatise and a Bible study...

Paragraph 2: Eric wished her happiness. She was, after all, he wrote with a certain degree of lightness, "freed from all sacred vows in light of the new findings"...*It was true then. He knew about Ty!*

Paragraph 3: Eric would see her briefly, having promised her mother he would check on her en route home from an assignment in "an as-yet-unspecified remote area in the Arctic Circle." Date, no later than December 25—perhaps sooner—so Merry Christmas!

Just as shackles of a guilt-ridden childhood fell off...just as Eric declared himself in unique way...just as she made ready to share with him the secret spot in the stratosphere where storm clouds never gathered and temperature never changed...she, Lauren, and he, Eric, were torn apart again by "others" just as they had always been.

But something—no, some*one*—much higher than the secret mountaintop—held her together. The Unseen Hand seemed to press an efficiency button preparing her for the new crisis. As if lights flashed simultaneously, Lauren saw the words *Eric is coming* here. Eric is the investigator that Ty wishes to avoid. Eric thinks I am to marry Ty. And finally, *Eric is involved in a "Bible study."* Which—or could it be all?—of these had Nella referred to as the change in his life which made his world "all but change orbits"?

With a newfound strength which surprised her, Lauren went down to dinner. At the pleasant meal nobody made mention of the Petrov couple or of Ty's date of departure.

"Are tomorrow's plans finalized?" Nella asked.

"Beautifully," Troy said, "thanks to your niece."

Lauren thanked him and, catching her aunt's eye, nodded in the direction of the wing the women occupied. Excusing herself, Lauren left before after-dinner coffee. Nella followed her down the hall.

"Come to my room," Lauren suggested. "I have letters from Eric which raise questions—questions which only you can answer."

Nella nodded as if she understood. Then, taking the letters, she scanned them calmly one by one. "Never mind my questions. Let's get to yours," she said, laying the last one aside.

"What does Eric mean, Nella—about our not being related—?" At the sound of her words, Lauren faltered.

"It's that simple—and a crying shame that somebody didn't straighten the two of you out long ago! But," she spread her hands wearily, "maybe the Lord intended that I should be the one. You're a big girl now—so, are you ready for this?"

"I'm ready."

Nella talked rapidly, and the story she told, although totally other-directional, was as incredible as Jessica's.

There were times when Lauren wanted to cry out and other times when she wished to question, to challenge...protect...defend. But she sat stoically listening. This, she knew, was the revelation she had waited for all the painful years that made up her life since the Day of Discovery.

Eric's mother, Erica Powell, had been in love with Lauren's father, Cory Eldridge, since high school days. The wedding day was set for the "perfect marriage," according to their families and friends.

"Then something happened to Erica which changed her life completely. She fell ill just a week before the wedding and had to have emergency surgery—the kind that makes it impossible for a woman to conceive. Oh, Cory took it fine. Not Erica! She refused to think she was lovable, turning her back on Cory and the rest of the world."

"You mean—" The little gasp came in spite of Lauren's efforts for control.

"I *mean* that it would have been imposible for your father and Erica to be Eric's parents. Want me to go on?"

"Yes," Lauren whispered, wondering how the story could possibly end. Wondering, too, how Eric had received the devastating news.

The couple went their separate ways, Nella went on. In their senior year of college, Cory met Lauren's mother, Roberta Trusdale—the freckled, good-humored, and undemanding girl who was Erica's exact opposite. "She was overwhelmed like—"

"Like I was—when Ty noticed me?" The words stung in Lauren's throat.

"Only you know your feelings, Lauren. But, yes,

I would compare the two of you.

"Erica, supposedly in a fit of pique, married Fred Thorne. But it was a tragic mistake, Oh, maybe it *could* have worked if Erica had made any effort." Nella shook her head sadly and was silent.

"But—but Eric? Who *is* he?" The question was wrenched from her.

Her aunt inhaled deeply. "It all reads like a novel," she said at last. "Erica became neurotic in her wild desire to bear a child. The doctor finally suggested an adoption—an idea which she rejected. No way would she accept an 'outsider,' she said. And then her twin sister, Eula, who married a naval officer, died in childbirth—"

"Eric?" Lauren whispered the name.

"Eric," Nella said. "But there is more. Incredible as it sounds, Eric's biological father was also Fred Thorne's brother. He was killed in Vietnam and never saw the child. I don't expect you to absorb all this at one sitting."

Lauren felt as if sleep had released her from her body. She was walking around in a dream. Soon she would return and the world would be as she had left it.

"He—Eric—is their nephew, their—how can I say it? Their *double* nephew—Uncle Fred's and Aunt Erica's."

"Yes, as close kin as one can get short of his own parents, I guess. There's some money, Lauren, quite a large sum—"

But Lauren was not listening. Her aunt was right: She was unable to absorb this. Erica's words came back from the cave of her childhood memory: "...and it's so unfair when Eric's not even *his*." It had seemed, in view of the love scene they had witnessed, that Lauren's father was Eric's father also.

"Why didn't they tell us? Why did they let us go on thinking—the worst?"

"Part of what you thought was true, Lauren. You have to live with that. It's not a pretty story. But it's past. We have to move on out." When her aunt paused, Lauren nodded, and then Nella continued, "And they didn't tell you Eric's background partly to cover, I suspect. But don't be too hard on them."

Hard on them? I was never judgmental. It's what they did to us...

"But it went deeper, Lauren. Don't underestimate the four of them. They loved you dearly, and they understood you. You were strange children—strange and wonderful! The knowledge would have destroyed you both."

And this was better? We thought then that adults were a peculiar lot...we still think so...Eric and I...they let US bear the burden...

"You would have been hurt—you were so sensitive. And Eric would have run away, I suspect. That's the way you were as children."

"Maybe," Lauren said slowly as if waking up from her dream, "maybe we haven't changed much—"

"Oh, but you have! You've both made 180-degree turns. Eric did escape into Mexico, but he came back. He and Fred are together again—closer than ever before. Now, if he can just handle the new Lauren!"

"But he thinks I'm engaged to Ty. Jessica told him."

"Then let him get in the ring and fight!" Nella exploded. "There are two ways to climb an oak tree, you know—roll up your pant legs and scale the trunk or sit on an acorn and wait for it to grow!''

Kissing her gently, Nella moved toward the door, then hesitated. ''You knew that Eric wants to carry his 'preservation' program farther—or did you? Physically and spiritually. When he stops by, he will have completed a survey on pollution up North and throughout the rest of the state. But there's more— well, he'll tell you about his calling to do something about the poverty and illiteracy among the Mexican children. Mexico,'' she said dreamily, ''land of the coconut palms, trade winds, and sunshine—*so* warm!'' With a significant smile, her aunt opened the door. ''Berta told me this. Good night, baby.''

''Wait! Don't go! Is it true that you and Dr. Piriot plan to be married too?''

''We do, indeed! But, Lauren, why the *too?*'' She blew a kiss and was gone.

Why *did* she say it? Unable to sleep, but unable to think, Lauren lay still gazing at what must be the ceiling.

Exhausted from endless nights of sleeplessness and the constant rising and falling of emotions, Lauren dressed quickly in the early hours of the morning. December 21, the day of the winter solstice! This was to be a day of happiness, a day of joy, a day for culminating all the wonderful things that had happened to the children of the village. Lauren felt a strange mixture of exhilaration and apprehension.

''Today,'' she told her pale, almost-ethereal reflection in the mirror, ''will do more than culminate the experiences for the villagers. It must end my stay.''

Chapter Fourteen

Outside the inn there was commotion. "The men are having trouble getting the snowmobiles started," Nella said. "It must be 100 below out there."

"And there's nothing between the wind and the North Pole but a barbed wire fence!" Dr. Piriot said as he came into the front room. "Nella, see that Lauren dresses properly. It would be useless to tell her to stay home."

"That goes for all of us, including Ty," Nella answered.

"He is not to go!" the doctor growled.

Nella shrugged. "Tell *him* that." Then, turning to Lauren, "I've heated bricks and Tuk's wrapping them. We'll pile them into the snowmobiles for extra warmth. And we'll take extra blankets."

Troy interrupted from the door. "We have both machines going, but reluctantly so. We shall just hope—" His voice trailed off as Ty, ahead of the others, honked a horn impatiently.

Once outside, Lauren realized that perhaps her aunt's report on the temperature may have been accurate. Frigid air such as she had never known seeped through her clothes, its icy fingers clutching at her throat. It was almost impossible to breathe. Thankfully, she sank into the first of the snowmobiles, only vaguely aware that she sat between Troy, who drove and Ty. It seemed unimportant in face of the primitive urge to survive the Arctic's cold.

The trip up to the village was like a frozen dream. At long last Lauren saw a fuzzy light in the distance, its faint beams seeming to float crazily in a slanting sheet of snow crystals that cut through her wool scarf.

"Kakalota," she tried to whisper, but the word froze on her lips. The remainder of the unforgettable day took on an aura of unreality. *I shouldn't have allowed myself to get so tired,* Lauren thought as her weightless body seemed to react rather than feel.

Crowds knotted inside and outside the mission school. Mrs. Tulook, who had mastered English fairly well, was able to communicate with Indian and Eskimo groups as well as the later-arriving caravan of families from the airport community. She had a poorly ventilated fire burning in the seldom-used pit in the corner of the school. The room felt overheated.

"Must keep burning for to keep warm shark chowder and cooking reindeer meats." Mrs. Tulook grinned broadly at Lauren as she fanned the fire. "Men be lots hungry when games and races finish."

Almost choking with smoke at times, Lauren helped the children dress and rehearse their parts for erection of the Christmas story totem pole. Her hands felt stiff and cold. When Troy offered to help, she gladly relinquished her post and, pulling on her hooded parka, hurried across to the trading post to watch a blanket toss which was in progress outside. Some of the village women had gathered to watch their men being bounced high above the heavy blanket which strong hands of other men gripped. Yet it was not the ritual Lauren watched in fascination, but the look of sheer admiration and pride in the faces of the wives cheering their mates to greater and more dangerous heights.

When Troy joined her, Lauren said, "I think I have learned a lot about marriage from observing these people—how undemanding and devoted they are to each other, and how loving they are to their children."

Troy bent low to hear her words which the winds would have sucked away. She could feel his warm breath on her cheek. "For your book, my dear Lauren, or for yourself and your concept of marriage?"

Lauren turned her face away, letting the icy wind ruffle the fur around her face. "I will check Charlie's gifts," she said vaguely. "I've neglected Mother shamefully—and I will be getting back home soon."

"So it's true what I hear? You are going? But, then, you made it abundantly clear from the start. Dear Lauren," Troy grasped her arm, "listen to me! There's a saying that once you've come here, you can never go all the way home. If ever you should—"

Not trusting her voice, Lauren pulled away and ran the short distance to the trading post. The air inside was dank and musty. When her eyes adjusted to the darkness, Lauren looked at some pieces of ivory. Mother would like the cameo.... As she was about to pay Charlie, her eyes fastened on a new set of color postcards. On the very top was a picture of a lovable polar bear cub. "This too," she said quickly. It was almost noon. After the meal came erection of the totem pole, then dogsled races, followed by more food and folk dancing. The day she had looked forward to stretched out interminably long.

"Pardon me. Did you drop this, milady?"

There was no need to look at the speaker. Lauren would remember the voice forever.

"Thank you, Ty." Lauren accepted the card without meeting his eyes.

"Tee--chur! Tee--chur! Tully and Sak can't get feathers on. *Tee--chur!*" the children all seemed to be calling in one breath.

Lauren turned quickly toward the door, then, glancing at Ty's face for the first time, gasped. He was haggard, thin, and almost wasted in appearance. "Should you be here?"

Ty shrugged. "Should *you?*"

"I had to come—"

"So did I . Or can't you find it within yourself to believe that I could meet a commitment?"

"Don't, Ty—"

Ty moved between her and the door. "You didn't ask me why I came. Maybe you don't care at this point. Be that as it may, I wanted you to know that I'll never forget you and what you've done. I don't know what's come over me, but I'm staying to meet 'Mr. Clean.' "

"I *have* to go, Ty. Come with me if you wish. Mr. *who?*"

"This do-gooder, whoever he is. No need to burden you further with 'harboring a criminal,' 'aiding and abetting,' or whatever."

Outside the wind cut across their faces. When a sudden gust all but swept Lauren from her feet, Ty reached out to support her. "Aren't you proud of me?" he asked at the door of the mission. "My *nobility!*"

"Oh, Ty, I am! It's just that I'm tired, confused—"

Ty reached around her to open the door, his arm encircling her waist. She tried to pull away, but he held her close. "Think we'll meet again?"

Lauren pushed against the door. "I doubt it."

Ty's laugh sounded like the Ty of old—mocking—but today heartbreaking in her euphoric state of mind. "But nothing's impossible, you said."

"*Luke* said that, Ty. 'Nothing is impossible *with God*!' "

"We shall see." With a bow, he stepped back so Lauren could enter. "I haven't *reformed,* but if these children *are* sick...don't I sound maudlin? But we don't want to endanger your polar bears, now do we?"

Lauren did not look back to see if Ty followed her inside. Even as she helped the children adjust feathers and answer their countless questions, her mind churned with questions. *Why had Ty bothered to tell her that he would see the inspector? And why had he come here to tell her?*

Suddenly her hand flew to her face, causing some of the paint she was holding for one of the children to spill down the front of her parka. As she peeled the parka off, another part of her repeated the question that had caused her to spill the paint. Only it wasn't a question at all: It was the inevitable. *The inspector that Ty decided to face was—it HAD to be—Eric!* Outside a chant began, "Totem pole, totem pole!"

The onlookers shouted as Lauren herded the children ahead, and with them pushed against the wind. It was hard to walk. It was hard to hear the words that Troy, their beloved "Master," spoke. It was almost impossible to see...her imagination had to be running wild...but at the edge of the crowd—there floated a familiar face...opaque eyes in a deeply tanned face, solemn and unsmiling. Swaying on her feet, Lauren tried to close her eyes and her heart. One thought persisted: *We've never met in winter...*

In the days preceding the winter solstice celebration, Lauren had been too preoccupied to give any thought to how the totem pole could be erected. Now she stood watching in fascination as the men fastened heavy chains onto the top to form a block and tackle. Once finished, they stepped aside. The children, she saw, were to complete the job. Otherwise the entire project would have no meaning.

The protective instinct in her made Lauren long to rush forward and plead that the pole was too heavy for the small hands that carved its figures. But that would be all wrong. It was a part of their culture; it was a ritual, and more—it was a desire on the part of the adults to let their young prove themselves.

Grasping the straps at the end of the chain, the children waited for a signal. Lauren jumped when the blast of a gun split the air.

"Pull!" Sak, the 12-year-old in charge, ordered. The children responded, pulling and straining until their dark eyes appeared ready to pop from their sockets. Their hands would be blistered, bodies bruised. Surely the pole would fall and the children would be hurt or killed. Then, reassuringly, she heard, "Pull!"

When at last the pole, tall and beautiful, rose like a spire almost 80 feet above the frozen tundra, a jubilant shout went up from the crowd.

Lauren herself felt an unexplainable thrill of triumph—for the children and their parents, for the work she had helped them to complete, and for something more. It was a gladness in which she, like the other adults, had been able to stand aside, supporting but not shielding. It was a whole new concept of love. She felt fulfilled—complete.

The hours which had seemed to hover interminably suddenly picked up tempo, the hands on some clock inside her moving too fast. Excited children clamored for teacher's attention...groups closed in around her to discuss mealtime plans...and she *would* be taking part in the "Dog Mushing," would she not?

Lauren heard the words and answered them. But all the while her eyes were searching the throngs of people who seemed to be clustered everywhere. *Where was the face—the wonderful face—belonging to the only one with whom she could share her feeling of independence? Or was it dependence? On God—and on herself through the strength he had provided in such a strange way.*

She nibbled at the king salmon Nella brought to her and responded to a thousand "Chee-CHA-kos," glad that she had mastered an Alaskan "Hello." She was about to say yes to a bearded man in a plaid jacket who invited her to ride with him in the dogsled race when Dr. Piriot intervened.

"I am sorry, sir, but Miss Eldridge has another matter to attend to."

"What is it?" Lauren whispered to him.

"Your health! Use your head, my child. You're running out of time!"

With that strange warning, the doctor joined Nella. The two of them, rosy with excitement and the cold air, jumped into a sled. Other couples, one of them Jessica and Troy, gathered to enter the race while the dogs snarled at one another in undisguised hatred.

The afternoon wore on, and once Lauren was almost sure she caught sight of Eric again. But his back was turned to her and he was deep in conversation. She tried to make her way through the crowds watching the "dog mushing," but by the time she reached the spot where she thought he stood, it was Ty's face she saw—Ty and one of the village girls who was apparently about to be his partner in the race.

Ty caught her eye. There was a strange, unreadable expression in his dark eyes, and the little "all's well" circle of his right index finger joining his thumb was puzzling. So what if he chose to make another conquest? Ty was Ty. Life to him meant excitement—one big adventure after another—no more "smuggling" in of potentially hazardous materials, maybe...she could hope for that...and somehow she knew that the victory sign had meant more than a taunt.

Lauren realized suddenly that there was no feeling in her legs. Maybe that accounted for her sense of unreality, as if her disembodied spirit floated freely, no longer bound by the laws of gravity.

Was this one of the warning signals that Dr. Piriot had mentioned? She couldn't remember as her mind too felt numbed by the prolonged exposure to cold. Trying to maintain her balance, Lauren made her way to the door of the mission, grateful to find it deserted.

Once inside, she peeled off her parka and boots with fingers blue from exposure. Finding no hot water, she poured some of the still-warm coffee into a basin and soaked her feet and hands. Gradually spots of color returned to her hands, and with return of circulation came the overpowering nausea she had come to expect.

But to her dismay no color appeared in either foot—not even a white spot when she pushed the purplish flesh with hopeful fingers. Should the feet be elevated or allowed to dangle? *Oh, why hadn't she listened? How could she have been so casual?*

There should be a pair of woolen socks in the closet that would fit. Troy kept a good supply in case the children needed to change into dry ones. Finding a pair that looked large enough, Lauren pulled her numb feet into them, noting that her ankles were beginning to swell. She must remember to tell the doctor that. Maybe he would be in soon—

Her thoughts were cut short when there was a peck on the window. Tully, the Indian lad who had grown to be one of Lauren's favorites, motioned for her to look where he was pointing. There, at the back of the building, the children in their eagerness for their very own ice-block race were wrapping the great chunks of ice in preparation for racing down the slope once the adult games drew to a close.

Lauren watched, smiling and waving, as word went from ear to ear that Teacher was at the window. Even as she stood the few minutes, the pain in her legs worsened. What would happen in a case like this? The thought frightened her.

Outside, the late afternoon had darkened. There would be no sunrise, no matter how low, to help lighten this strange world on the day of the winter solstice. Lights would be on where the games were in progress, but Lauren preferred the solitude that the darkness afforded. Somehow it came as no surprise when a voice spoke from behind her. Surely, she thought later, she must have sensed another presence.

"So—school okay?" The voice was as powerful as she remembered, its deep gravel-tone giving strength to the gaunt, adolescently-thin frame of the speaker. Summers were back. Childhood was back. She and Eric were taking up where they had left off.

"So-so. I'm no whiz kid like you." Last summer's conversation?

" 'For the wisdom of this world is foolishness with God.' "

"First Corinthians 3:19," Lauren responded automatically. "But you came in without knocking!"

"So I did." Eric's voice was barely audible above the howl of wind as it hurled its forces against the ancient walls and then complained of its bruises.

When they met like this at the beach, Eric and Lauren never met each other's gaze. They simply took up in midgame where they had left off. And, unless her mind was playing tricks, the same was true in the Arctic Northland. No! It was *more* than true..it was a miracle...one that could only happen here where blue-white shadows said that nothing ever really dies, but simply changes shape with the passage of time... buried in the snow, carried by the wind, or shining like starfish in a turquoise sky.

If I look, he might change shapes—blow away— Oh, Eric, not this time! Don't vanish in the vapors of my imagination—

But the warm voice was very real. "Lauren," it said, "I love you!"

And the floating spirit that was Lauren replied, "Eric, I love you too."

Then, before they would reach each other, nature intervened. At first there was only a flicker of light. Then there was a blinding flash. Someone must have turned on the lights, invading her wonderful moment with Eric. No, the flashes—for there were more—were too brilliant. The northern lights!

Eric must know. She must tell him. But Lauren was too wonder-filled to speak. Words had never been necessary for the two of them. Eric would know. Eric knew everything—even that he should take her hand and hold it while a million rainbows of brilliant reds and greens, like Christmas-tree lights, swooped and swirled across the blackness of the Alaskan sky...shooting golden arrows that raced from one corner of the room to the other, pinning the two of them together... lighting up Eric's beloved face as he bent slowly toward her to touch her lips with a first gentle kiss.

Eric seemed to be fighting against the impulse to hold her closer. Why should he? With warm abandon, Lauren wound her arms around his neck and gave herself completely to the strength of his loving arms, the sweetness of his more-demanding kiss until, as softly as they had begun, the ripples of color faded to soft pastels. And then there was darkness again.

"The aurora borealis," Lauren dared to breathe when Eric released her. "Oh, Eric, how fitting it should come tonight!"

"Don't! Oh, please don't, Lauren," he groaned.

Lauren recoiled. The old Eric was back—the one

who was in control...who made all the rules. Before
she could ask what could stand between them now,
Eric spoke in the all-too-familiar voice. "Spectacular,
wasn't it? Scientists believe the phenomenon is caused
by charged particles from the sun bombarding the
earth's atmosphere—"

"Oh, Eric, I don't *care* what caused the lights! I only
care that we love each other. *Why* did you pull away
when everything's all right for us now? When we're
free to love—"

"Free to love?" Eric's voice was hoarse with suffering. "You aren't free at all! Why, *why* didn't you
tell me about him?"

Relief spread over her entire being. "Ty? I can
explain—"

But there was not time. Again nature, whose whims
man has been unable to control, intervened. But this
time not with shimmering scarves of light, but with
a far greater force.

First there was an explosion. Louder than thunder.
More earthshaking. Violent! Lauren had never expected to witness a breaking away of a glacier section,
but instinctively she knew that one was occurring.
Calving, the natives called it.

There was no time for words—just time to grasp
Eric's hand and stand looking with him in horrified
silence at what appeared to be a wall of ice just yards
away—plunging downward to destroy everything within its path in its hurry to the sea.

The children. The children were in its wake! There
was not even time to tell Eric they were there, ready
for their ice-block race while their unknowing parents
had gone on with their games.

There were horrified screams. Lauren, in her frozen state, saw only a wild confusion of deadly ice and small bodies tossed into the air. Only one face did she recognize in that horrible moment—*Sak!*

Whispering a prayer, she rushed with Eric through the door of the mission well ahead of the others.

Eric forced his way through the labyrinth of tortured structure left by the passing ice sheet. Lauren followed close behind, aware of the freezing cold against her thin clothing, but not caring.

Reaching to push her wind-whipped hair from her face, Lauren lost her bearings. Then there was human sound. Not much. Just a moan. But enough to tell her there was life.

"Tee--chur...Tee--chur..." the faint voice faded.

Almost paralyzed with cold, she tried to follow the sound, only to become more confused. *Eric! Where was Eric?*

There was a second explosion—more violent than before. It was then that Lauren's legs gave way and she crumpled beneath a sheet of snow and ice. It was strangely warm. And nothing seemed to matter anymore.

There was a distant hum of voices. "Here she is... dead? No—breathing faintly...will she make it, Doc? Emergency! Legs paralyzed...hypothermia...looks like pre-gangrene. The other one? Lost...buried...hopeless..." *Eric! Eric was dead. She was dying. That was good. Only they would never make it to their mountaintop and go into the Long Sleep together...*

Time lost all meaning. Hours, days, maybe years later she was floating in space. The voices died away. And then there was merciful darkness...

★ ★ ★

There was a blaze of shimmering lights. Strange, because her eyes were closed. But behind her eyelids there were faces and places, none of them familiar.

"Oh, here we are! Welcome back," a starched voice was saying. "Just enter slowly. It will all come back when the anesthesia wears off. Can you count for me?"

Of course she could count—in English, in Greek, and up to 100 in Spanish.

The same voice soothed her, "You're Lauren, remember? And soon you're going to move your legs. I'm your nurse, Nurse Larkin."

*She had a nurse. Her nurse had a name. And she had legs...*that seemed to be significant.

"Wake up, Lauren! Move your legs. The specialist managed to save them. You've had a sympathectomy— a cutting of the nerves to let the blood flow—stay awake now! You're in the hospital in Seattle.

Seattle...Seattle...a long time ago...

"That's it! *Think!* There was a glacial storm that did a lot of damage. Are you hearing? Oh—so you want to hear more? *He* can tell you." The nurse continued, "Come on, Lauren, open your eyes for me— you're going to have company!"

She must have mouthed the word because Nurse Larkin said softly, "The man who's going to marry you, he says! Ah, yes, some young man you've got there... gave equal time to your room and the chapel yonder."

Marry? Did the nurse say marry?

Behind her eyelids the faces of three men came into focus. One so gently you hardly knew it was there. The other exotic, commanding attention. And the third?

Familiar, but always shifting directions, moving the tides, like stars that twinkled on through millions of light years... She had sent two of the men away. And the other?

Slowly she felt her eyelids flutter. "Plenty of time to do what needs doing," Nurse Larkin encouraged.

Lauren struggled to shift her eyes to the door, but there was a warning stab of pain in her head. "Careful!" Nurse Larkin cautioned. "We'll see him. Just be patient. He's a hero, this young man of yours—rushing in like that to save the little boy!"

Sak...an explosion...bodies...screams...a shudder shook her body.

"Good! You're remembering—and there'll be so much to talk about. This one wasn't the only hero, you know. There were two other men—quite a story! Maybe these will help—see the lovely ivory cross? And isn't *he* a dear, this cuddly stuffed polar bear? But what*ever* are you going to do with one dozen crates of oranges?"

Nurse Larkin asked, "Are you ready for the impatient young man? He's threatening to break the door down—some feat, and him with two broken legs!"

Her fragmented thoughts were interrupted by two sharp raps on the door. And as if there had been no time between, Lauren asked weakly, "Who's there?"

"The Almighty!"

First. Last. And always. Revelation 1:8. Alpha and Omega of Love...

Then, aloud, in a clear, steady voice, she said, "Come in without knocking, Eric, my darling. Come in for that Eskimo kiss!"